The Bewitching Of AVELINE JONES

For Janna, my dark half

First published in the UK in 2021 by Usborne Publishing Ltd., Usborne House, 83-85 Saffron Hill, London EC1N 8RT, England, usborne.com

Usborne Verlag, Usborne Publishing Ltd., Prüfeninger Str. 20, 93049 Regensburg, Deutschland, VK Nr. 17560

Illustrations copyright © Usborne Publishing Ltd., 2021

Illustrations by Keith Robinson.

Cover typography by Sarah J Coleman/inkymole.com

The name Usborne and the Balloon logo are Trade Marks of Usborne Publishing Ltd.

A CIP catalogue record for this book is available from the British Library.

JFMAM JASOND/21 ISBN 9781474972154 05658/1

Printed and bound in Great Britain by CPI Group (UK) Ltd, Croydon, CR0 4YY

MIX
Paper from
responsible sources
FSC® C020471

The Bewitching Of AVELINE JONES

Phil Hickes

Illustrated by Keith Robinson

USBORNE

"Witches can rayse stormes
and tempests in the air."

Daemonologie,
King James I of England and VI of Scotland.

Chapter 1
Stone and Glass

Aveline Jones glared at the thorny bramble lodged in the sleeve of her T-shirt. Wincing, she freed herself from its spiky grip. This was the most ridiculously overgrown garden she'd ever stepped foot in. Sighing, she took off her grimy glasses and wiped them on her T-shirt. She would be staying here for the next couple of weeks, so supposed she'd better get used to it.

Aveline's mum worked for a charity and had been so busy recently that Aveline had abandoned hopes of actually going away for a summer holiday. But then, with just enough time for a break before school started back up in September, her mum had announced that she'd booked them a cottage in the countryside, not too far from Bristol where they lived. Aveline would have preferred two weeks on a beach in Spain, but this was better than nothing. So while her friends were probably swimming in a perfect blue ocean somewhere, here she was, having a fight with a blackberry bush.

However, there was one very good reason why Aveline was willing to risk injury to reach the end of the garden.

The Witch Stones.

There was an ancient stone circle, right here in Norton Wick, the village where they were staying. The name gave Aveline the shivers. Ghosts, ghouls and witches were, of course, her specialist subject, and this creepily named stone circle had been mentioned in a book she'd read once. Now she would be able to visit it for real. Apparently, the stones had been here for thousands of years but, as far as Aveline could tell, nobody *really* knew why the circle had been built, though there were a lot of theories.

Some said it was a type of calendar, so ancient people could keep track of the seasons. Others said it was a temple, where people might come and worship the gods. There were those who claimed that aliens had built it. Others said it was connected to the druids, ancient Celtic priests who were either healers, wizards or bloodthirsty fiends, depending on who you believed.

Aveline found it all very interesting, but it was the *name* of these stones that really fascinated her. The book she'd read hadn't mentioned anything about witches, so why were they called The Witch Stones? The first step in finding the answer would be to see them for herself, and the owner of the cottage had told them that the stones were *very* close by. Right at the end of the garden, in fact.

Steeling herself for more scratches from the vindictive blackberry thorns, Aveline fought her way onwards. She would have thought someone might have tidied the place up before they'd arrived. Plants and weeds thrust themselves skyward, blocking her path at every turn. Sparrows and thrushes scuttled in the undergrowth. Huge spiders bobbed between the bushes on gossamer threads. Bees buzzed busily between the bright flowers, pollen coating their little legs like fuzzy yellow leg warmers. It felt as if she'd stepped uninvited into a private party.

Following a nasty encounter with some nettles, and a brief scuffle with a hawthorn bush, Aveline was making good progress when her foot hit something hard that made a clinking sound. Bending down, she rummaged around in the undergrowth. Light glinted off something in the dark soil. Intrigued, she dug her fingers into the earth until they closed on something solid. Burrowing deeper, she prised the object loose.

A bottle.

Old by the looks of it, with a thin neck and small oval body. Its glass was green and murky and impossible to see through, even after she'd cleaned off the clods of dirt. Straightening up, Aveline held it to the sunlight. Her fingers tingled, but that could just have been nettle stings. Inside she could see *something*, but it was hard to tell exactly what that *something* was. Just a blackish blob. All the same, it gave her the chills; a ripple of unease crept up her arms.

Giving the bottle a shake, she heard a tiny rattle. Examining the neck of the bottle more closely, she saw that it had been sealed with a thick layer of wax, which might have once been red but was now the colour of tar. She tried pulling it loose, but it was as hard as cement. It seemed that if she wanted to see what the bottle contained, she would probably have to smash it – something she was reluctant to do. In fact, part of her wanted to leave it well alone. But she was curious, too. Old bottles with things inside them couldn't just be ignored.

Holding it between finger and thumb, Aveline finally found her way to the bottom of the garden and placed it

carefully at the base of
the stone wall that
separated their cottage
from the fields beyond.
A huge rhododendron
bush offered some
welcome shade and so she
sat down beside it to catch
her breath. A few minutes here in
the earthy coolness would be a welcome relief from the
mugginess of the late afternoon. August had been
blisteringly hot and even though they were nearly at the
end of the month, it showed no sign of cooling down.

Rubbing the scratches on her arms, Aveline glanced
back at the cottage. They'd arrived an hour or so ago,
along with a small mountain of supplies. Being in a new
place felt disorientating. The view was different. The
smells were different. Everything was different. And
she'd certainly never stayed anywhere quite so remote
before. The village had been hard to find, tucked away
down twisting, narrow lanes. With its crooked houses and
weathered signposts, it felt as if the world had moved on
but forgotten to tell the residents. That had been one of
the reasons why her mum had wanted to come here –

she'd thought it would be fun for them to get away from the bustle of the big city. Well, she'd certainly got her wish, Aveline thought with a smirk. Not only had they got away from the city but it felt like they'd stepped back in time. There were unsightly brown stains on the cottage walls. The taps dripped. The roof leaked. The windowpanes were cracked. The place was like an old man with creaky joints and a nasty cough. Aveline had been relieved to discover it had electricity and hot water. But it did make her wonder – when had anyone last stayed here? It felt like they were the first people to enter the place for a hundred years.

Feeling a little cooler now, Aveline clambered to her feet and spotted a small wooden gate in the garden wall. Just like everything else here, it had seen better days. The green paint had faded and blistered and the lock was brown with rust. With a loud grunt, Aveline tugged the bolt free and pushed the gate open, the screech of its hinges a sure sign that it hadn't been opened in a long time.

Immediately, her eyes widened.

In front of her was a ring of gigantic, moss-covered stones. She'd found them – The Witch Stones – almost within touching distance of where they were staying.

Aveline had wondered if she might have to pay to go and see them, but here they were in all their glory, with no car parks, ticket booths, information stands or other visitors to be seen. It felt like she'd stumbled into a secret place, hidden away in the green folds of the countryside.

Stepping closer, Aveline sniffed the warm summer air. Her first impression was that the stones smelled of cow dung. But then there *was* a herd of cows milling around, so that made perfect sense.

She counted thirteen stones in total, double-checking to make sure. Three stones stood upright, shaped like giant arrowheads – gigantic chunks of rock that looked as if they weighed a thousand tonnes each. The other stones lay flat in the grass, their scarred, grey expanses like the backs of huge whales when they surface for the briefest moment.

Aveline stared with her mouth gaping, immediately fascinated by this eerie monument. It did seem a little strange that she was the only one here, especially as it was the peak of the summer holidays. In fact, the only other living things to be seen were the cows, which wandered idly between the stones, munching on the lush summer grass while swatting away flies with their tails.

She considered the situation. The stones were certainly in a remote location. And while impressive, they weren't anywhere near as grand as the giant megaliths at Stonehenge, which attracted coachloads of tourists from all over the world. Maybe it was simply because these weren't as famous? Anyway, she didn't mind one bit. It meant she would have them all to herself.

Then she heard laughter. Maybe the stones did have another visitor after all?

Suddenly shy, Aveline retreated back through the wooden gate and hunkered down in the foliage of the cottage garden, leaving the gate open so she could still see the stones. The day had a hazy, fuzzy feel about it now, everything starting to soften like melting butter. The horizon shimmered. Midges danced lazily between the sun's rays.

As Aveline watched with heavy eyes, a figure emerged through the haze. A girl. Dressed in a flowing white dress, which contrasted with her long black hair, she tiptoed through the long grass as if following the steps of some ancient ritual, trailing her hands over the stones and stroking them like a cat. Aveline couldn't tear her eyes away, transfixed by the girl's curious movements.

What on earth was she doing?

As Aveline stared, the girl paused, then shot a look in her direction, a glint of a smirk flashing across her dark

features. Aveline had thought she'd done a good job of concealing herself, but the girl appeared to have known instantly that she was being observed. Embarrassed, Aveline shrank back further into the long grass. It wasn't good to be caught staring.

Grabbing the bottle she'd found a few minutes earlier, she traced her way back through the garden as quickly as she could, cursing as the brambles tried to grab her again. Running into the cottage kitchen, she pulled herself up on the edge of the sink and peered out of the window, but although she could just about see the stones through the open gate, the girl had disappeared.

"You know what curiosity did to the cat, Aveline," her mum said from behind her.

"Stopped it dying from boredom?" Aveline snapped, jumping down.

Her mum laughed, tossing the curls back from her face.

"Oh, come on, Aveline, it's not *that* bad here. What were you looking at?"

"I went and found the stone circle and I was going to have a look around but there was a girl there."

"Well, maybe she's a kindred spirit – she might be as fascinated by those stones as you are. You should have gone and said hello—"

"Mum," Aveline said, cutting her off before she had a chance to get into one of her *you should immediately make friends with everyone you see* conversations.

"Anyway, what's that horrible dirty thing on the nice, clean counter?" Aveline's mum said, taking her cue to change the subject.

"I found it in the garden. It's an old bottle. But I don't know what's in it, because it's sealed shut."

"Well, I'd rather it stayed in the garden."

"But there might be something valuable in there!" Aveline protested.

"Yes, there might also be nasty germs. If it's been in the garden for a long time then I'm sure it can survive a few more days out there."

Aveline was about to argue, but then remembered that they were supposed to be having a relaxing time, so she picked the bottle up and opened the back door.

"Okay, I won't be a minute."

The warm breeze fanned her face. Gingerly, she made her way down through the garden again, being careful not to trip with the bottle in her hand. Once at the wall, she peered out through the gateway at the stones, wondering if the girl was still there, but apart from the cows the site appeared to be deserted. Reaching down, she placed the bottle carefully in the soil, scooping a few handfuls of earth round it to keep it from toppling over. Her mum was right. If it had been buried out here for this long, it'd be fine until she decided what to do with it. And actually, Aveline wasn't sure she wanted it in the cottage either. Something felt…off about it, so perhaps she should do some research first before she did anything else. Her friend, Harold, would definitely be able to help. She'd met him last year and his great-uncle owned a bookshop. Harold was coming to stay with them for a few days and he might be able to dig up a book about old bottles that he could bring with him. She made a mental note to speak to him before he arrived.

As she stood back up, a large magpie landed on the garden wall.

"Shoo," Aveline said. "Go away and mind your own business."

In her head she heard the start of a familiar rhyme:

One for sorrow, two for joy…

She couldn't remember the rest. Meanwhile, the magpie had ignored her command and stared at her with its beady black eyes. Opening its wings, it let out a raucous caw that sounded uncannily like mocking laughter – or a cackling witch.

A witch for The Witch Stones.

As if hearing her thought, the magpie wheeled away, landing on the tallest of the stones before cawing once again. Aveline turned her back on it and ran up to the cottage.

Just before she reached the door, something made her turn around for one final look. Standing on tiptoe, for a second she thought she saw a silhouette crouched in the gateway, staring up at the cottage. Aveline didn't wait to see who it belonged to. The shadows were creeping up the path and she hurriedly shut the door behind her, taking care to slide home the lock.

"Some of the Norton Wick stones appear
to have been toppled deliberately,
possibly for superstitious reasons."

Archaeological Survey,
Norton Wick, 1953.

Chapter 2

The Watcher in the Circle

Aveline didn't have to wait long to see the mysterious girl again. The next morning she was lounging on the sofa when she heard the unmistakeable clip-clop of horse's hooves. She'd seen a few people riding horses along the narrow lanes and bridle paths since they'd arrived. It made a pleasant change from cars and buses. Curious, she clambered to her feet, opened the front door and made her way down the path to the gate.

A black horse trotted down the lane towards her, unlike any she'd seen before. Tall and sleek, the horse swung its head arrogantly, as if to confirm that it was indeed magnificent. Its flanks shone with sweat, emphasizing the outline of its muscles. As it tossed its shiny fringe out of its eyes, Aveline was momentarily reminded of her friend, Harold, and his floppy hair.

As the horse trotted closer, Aveline's attention switched to its rider, whose long and lustrous black hair matched the horse's mane. It was the same girl she'd seen the day before at the stones. Aveline had always thought horse riders were legally bound to wear helmets, just like motorcyclists, but the girl's hair trailed freely behind her like a black pennant flying from the turret of a castle. She wore leather riding boots, jodhpurs and a padded olive-green coat. She really did resemble some warrior queen from the pages of history, riding into battle at the head of her army. Suddenly terrified of being caught staring for the second day running, Aveline shrank back into the shadow of the apple tree that stood guard by their gate.

But it was too late.

Her stomach cramped with anxiety as the girl pulled on the horse's reins. Stamping its feet impatiently, the beast wheeled around and flashed Aveline a haughty glance. The sun flared behind horse and rider, making Aveline squint as she peered up at the black silhouette surrounded by golden rays. *Why can't I make grand entrances like that?* she thought. She usually ended up fumbling with doorknobs or tripping over her shoelaces.

As she stood there, shielding her eyes from the sun, she had a similar sensation to the evening before when she'd found the bottle. A tingle of electricity ran up her back and around her neck, as if she'd sidestepped into another world for a second. Shyly, she pushed up her glasses and raised her hand in a hesitant wave. The girl seemed to be sizing her up and it felt like a long time before she responded, but as the horse stamped again, the girl raised a gloved hand. A subtle gesture, but a friendly one.

Just as Aveline was considering saying something, the girl lightly pulled on the reins and the horse turned and continued trotting down the lane until they vanished around the corner. Taking a deep breath, Aveline followed cautiously. She didn't want to be caught spying again, but she did want to see where they went. But when she turned the corner, horse and rider had disappeared.

Which was odd.

She couldn't see them in the village high street. They wouldn't have had time to reach the far end, which made Aveline think they must have turned off somewhere. Idly, she continued to walk down towards the village shop, which she'd been in once already to buy sweets. It stocked fresh bread and eggs, cold meats and cider from the local farm, along with a few canned goods that looked like they'd been sitting on the shelves for years.

As she stood outside the shop, wondering whether to walk further down into the village, she heard the bell ring behind her as the door opened. Turning, she saw a bizarrely dressed person emerge. The woman was short, around the same height as Aveline, and broad, with a reddened, lined face, as if she spent a lot of time outdoors. Dressed in long flowing black robes, she wore heavy boots without laces, out of the top of which poked a pair of rainbow-coloured socks. Oddest of all, on her head she wore a bowler hat, which Aveline had only previously seen on pinstriped businessmen in black-and-white photographs.

"Morning to you," the woman exclaimed, taking her hat off for a minute to fan her face. "Phew, it's hotter than a monk's flip-flop out here."

Aveline smiled hesitantly.

"Don't believe we've met before," the woman said, speaking in a brisk, businesslike manner. "What brings you all the way out here to Norton Wick, may I ask?"

Aveline caught a whiff of something sweet and herbal. "My mum and I are here on holiday. From Bristol."

"I see. A welcome break from the big city, I'm sure, though I hope you don't find it too dull. Not many people your age live here, I'm afraid."

"Actually, I just saw a girl around my age riding a horse. I was wondering which direction she went in. Did you see her?"

The woman frowned. "Can't say I did. What did she look like?"

"Oh, long black hair. Pretty," Aveline said, blushing as she did.

"Just like you then, my dear," the woman said, which made Aveline warm to her. "But I'm not certain who that could be. I certainly can't recall seeing anyone like that riding a horse."

The woman trailed off, a far-away look in her eyes, before sticking out a grimy hand.

"I'm Alice, by the way, the vicar of Norton Wick. You must come and see me up at St Michael's sometime." Aveline must have looked blank, because Alice added, "St Michael's is the church. You can't miss it. Big stone building with stained-glass windows. You know, where they put all the dead people. It's close to the stones, just on the other side of the field. I assume you've visited our famous Witch Stones?"

"Yes, we're staying right by them," Aveline said, a note of pride in her voice.

"Well, good for you. I can't think of a better spot. Just

mind you don't pay any attention to any tall tales you might hear." Alice lowered her voice. "There are still people in the village who won't go near those stones once the sun has set."

"Really?" Aveline said, edging a little closer. This certainly sounded worth listening to.

"Oh, yes, local superstitions take a long time to die out around here," Alice continued in a conspiratorial whisper. "They're passed down from generation to generation. You know the sort of thing, I'm sure. Ghosts and ghouls and goblins. Evil faeries that'll snatch you away if you happen to linger there during a waning moon."

Aveline nodded. As it happened, she knew *exactly* what Alice was talking about.

"Mind you, I'd take it all with a pinch of salt if I were you. Most folk around here still think the moon is made of cheese. It wasn't that long ago they were busy—" Alice suddenly stopped herself mid-thought, shook her head and clamped her bowler hat back on her short salt-and-pepper hair. "Anyway, I must be off. I didn't catch your name by the way."

"Aveline. I'm here with my mum."

"Aveline and her mum. Righto. I shall remember you in my prayers."

They exchanged smiles and handshakes.

While she hadn't learned much, their brief conversation had added another touch of intrigue to the day. The Witch Stones were proving to be as mysterious as their name.

She deliberated about returning to the cottage or walking up a little further, to see if she could spot a house with stables. In the end, her curiosity won. Her mum knew she wouldn't wander off too far.

The houses down in the centre of the village were quite grand. Old, like the rest of the village, but owned by people who obviously had money. Large stone mansions with immaculate lawns and gravelled drives, on which were parked shiny BMWs and Mercedes. Some of these homes looked big enough to have stables, though Aveline didn't dare walk up the driveways. Satisfied that the girl must have ridden into one of these, Aveline wandered on, enjoying the warm hum of the late summer morning and the smell of freshly cut hay in the air. She passed the village green, beside which was the local pub, called The Moon & Sickle. The sign depicted a large standing stone, next to which a gaunt man with a long beard and white robes raised a sickle blade into the night air. Aveline realized that the man was intended to be a druid, one of the mysterious Celtic priests she'd read about. They often had long beards. More research into them could be useful if she wanted to find out more about the stone circle. Were they good or evil? Aveline had no idea. Another thing to add to Harold's list. The druid on this sign certainly appeared to be pretty sinister. The sign had been painted in black and silver, the artist doing a good job of making the stone appear eerie and a little threatening. It seemed to capture the moment before something horrible was about to happen. Despite the heat of the day, Aveline shuddered.

Further on, the houses became smaller, linked together in a terrace. After that, the village pretty much ended, the lane narrowed and the hedgerows rose up into steep leafy banks on either side of the road. Satisfied that she'd just about explored everything Norton Wick had to offer, Aveline returned to the cottage, where she found her mum sitting outside, sipping a cool drink.

"Find anything interesting?" Aveline's mum said. "There's some home-made lemonade in the fridge if you want some."

"There's not much to see," Aveline conceded. "I saw a girl on a horse, met the local vicar and walked past a pub with a creepy sign."

"Everything's creepy as far you're concerned, Aveline,"

her mum said. "Go on, get yourself a drink. Sounds like you've worked up a thirst."

Later, after a lazy day relaxing at the cottage, they'd eaten and Aveline had beaten her mum at cards. Then she went to her room and yawned long and loud. Being tired when you were on holiday didn't matter so much. It wasn't a school night and with her mum in no rush to get up and do anything in the mornings, she could sleep for as long as she wanted. Her room was small and cosy, her bed soft, and she had a perfect view of the stones from her window. Being late summer, the sun was only just setting, but it had decided to go out in a blaze of glory. The horizon glowed, as if an artist had squeezed blobs of tangerine, scarlet and pink onto a gigantic brush and swept it through the sky. The sweet smell of grass and hay perfumed her room like incense. Somewhere in the distance a tractor rumbled along, the farmer probably gathering up the last of the summer hay bales.

Sinking to her knees and resting her elbows on the windowsill, Aveline watched the sun disappear from view, enjoying the songs of the birds as they bid one another goodnight. A silhouette swooped low through the stones, but as she watched its flight, her eyes drifted to something else.

Someone else.

A figure stood in the centre of the stones. Although it wasn't yet fully dark, in the twilight it was impossible to make out who they were. Yet even though she couldn't see their face, Aveline had an uncanny feeling that they were looking directly at her. She stared for a minute or two, unsure if her eyes were deceiving her, as the figure stood rooted to the spot. For a moment she wondered if she'd mistaken one of the stones for a person, but no, the shape was unmistakeably human. Aveline's elbows slipped from the sill, and she reached slowly to draw the curtains across, never once taking her eyes off the figure. Once the curtains finally obscured her view, Aveline waited for a minute or two before slowly opening a small crack in them to peer through.

The figure had gone.

All she could see was a circle of stones, as solid and still as they had been for thousands of years.

"Ye shall not interpret
omens or tell fortunes."

Leviticus 19:26.

Chapter 3
Magic Tricks

"Hello, this is Malmouth Funeral Home, I'm afraid we can't come to the phone right now as we're all dead."

Aveline dropped the phone to her side, rolled her eyes, then put it back up to her ear.

"Harold, you idiot."

"Who is this Harold of whom you speak?"

"Okay, it was funny the first time but don't milk it. How did you know it was me?"

"Your number comes up on my uncle's phone."

"Oh. Of course."

Aveline had first met Harold when she'd gone to stay at her Aunt Lilian's in Malmouth. They'd been friends ever since. Harold could be highly annoying but underneath the bad jokes, the immaturity, the moodiness, the impatience and the rudeness, he was actually pretty cool. Although they'd only seen each other once since then, when Aveline had gone to see her aunt again, they texted most days and FaceTimed occasionally. Harold was coming to stay with them tomorrow and, although she'd never tell him, Aveline couldn't wait for him to arrive. Sometimes he felt like her invisible friend, so it would be nice to actually see him in the flesh.

"What's up then?" Harold said. "And how's the holiday cottage? I hope you've saved the best room for me."

"It's a bit old and creaky, to be honest. But the good news is that it's got a coal shed, so we've decided to put you in there. Dark, cold and dirty. You'll love it. How's your uncle, by the way?"

Harold shouted into the distance. "Aveline wants to know how you are!"

In answer there came a crackly old voice she knew and loved: Mr Lieberman, Harold's great-uncle. "Tell her that I'm very well and we're looking forward to seeing her when we come up tomorrow. Or is it the day after? I get so confused with dates. Anyway, please don't make foolish jokes when answering the bookshop phone,

36

Harold, there's a good boy. Professionalism at all times, please."

"He says he's fine," Harold said curtly. "What's Norton Wick like? Is there much to do?"

"Actually, you won't believe it, but our cottage is right next to a stone circle."

"Really?"

Harold actually sounded impressed, which pleased Aveline no end. Most of the time he pretended not to care about anything.

"Yeah. And you'll never guess what they're called... The Witch Stones."

"Uh-oh."

"Exactly. That's why I'm calling. I've got something I need you to do."

"I thought you were calling to see how I am."

"Don't be stupid."

"What is it then?"

"I found this old sealed bottle buried in the garden of the cottage, not far from the stones. It could have got there by accident, but I think someone put it there on purpose."

"What's in it?"

"Don't know yet."

"Well, what are you waiting for?"

"I can't open it without smashing it and I thought I should wait until we can find out more about it."

"Does it say Coca-Cola on it?"

"Harold, I'm serious. There's something a bit creepy about it. Just have a look through the bookshop, see if you can find any books about old bottles. And bring all the books you can find about stone circles. And Norton Wick. And druids. Oh, and anything about witches, too."

"Anything else? Or shall I just bring the whole bookshop?"

"Just see what you can find." Aveline put on a scary voice. "Our very lives may depend upon it, Harold."

"Okay, I'll have a root around."

"Thanks."

"See you soon then."

"Okay, bye."

"Bye."

Pleased that she'd packed Harold off to do some investigating, Aveline decided to wander over to the stones for an hour or so. Her mum didn't mind her going on her own – it was just like being out in the back garden, more or less – and she wanted to have a closer look. Not just because of last night, when she thought somebody was staring up at her window, but because of the local superstitions Alice the vicar had scoffed about, too. Also, she still had no idea why they were called The Witch Stones. Strange things had happened there though, she felt sure.

Checking that the bottle was still where she'd left it at the end of the garden, Aveline made her way through the gate and into the field. On the border of the circle stood a huge oak tree. Once autumn came, Aveline knew that its leaves would turn from green to orange embers and then a fiery red before gently floating down. Of all the seasons Aveline loved autumn the best. At times she wished she could wrap all its smells and colours up and wear them like a cloak. She'd had enough of the hot weather.

For a while she just wandered about, enjoying the sensation of being in this ancient place. Apart from a few cows mooching around, swishing their tails as they stared at her with idle curiosity, she was alone.

Or so she thought.

Just as she was examining one of the stones, she heard a voice from close behind her.

"Hello. Are you a witch?"

Turning, Aveline saw the mysterious girl she'd seen on the horse.

"N-no, I'm not," she stammered. Such an odd question. Was this girl trying to make fun of her?

"I know you're not really, I'm only joking," the girl said, her voice smooth as silk. "It's just that some say this place is a haven for witches, so I thought it best to check. Anyway, now I can see that you're far too pretty to be a witch."

Aveline felt herself blush. Pushing up her glasses, she smiled back at the girl. "Thanks."

As the girl stepped closer, Aveline noticed her unusual eyes: one an icy blue and the other a vivid emerald green. The girl's dark, sun-bronzed skin made them shine with a curious luminescence. Aveline had seen cats with odd coloured eyes before, but never a person. Combined with the girl's sleek black hair, they gave her a wild appearance and Aveline found herself a little envious.

"Anyway, witches only come out at night, everybody knows that," the girl continued. "If they go out in the sunlight they burst into flames and die horribly."

Aveline thought that only applied to vampires, but held her tongue, knowing that arguing about the finer points of the supernatural wasn't the best way to make friends.

"My name's Hazel. Hazel Browne. Browne with an *e*.

I saw you yesterday, didn't I?" the girl said with a directness that Aveline found slightly unnerving.

"Yes, you were on your horse. I'm Aveline. Um, Aveline with an *A*."

"Aveline! I love that name. I wish I was called that. At least you're not named after a nut. Though I suppose I should be grateful that I'm not called Pistachio or Macadamia."

Aveline laughed. The girl was funny. Not at all like she'd imagined her to be.

"So, what are you doing here among the stones, Aveline? Are you bored like me?"

"A bit. It is very quiet here – I'm still getting used to it. We're staying just over there," Aveline said, pointing in the direction she'd come from. "At the cottage with the green door."

Hazel clasped her hands together and stood up on her tiptoes to see. "Imagine that," she laughed. "Coming on holiday to Norton-middle-of-nowhere-Wick. Poor you. But at least your misery is my good fortune. It's going to be nice to have a friend at last."

A friend.

Aveline hitched up her jeans, straightened her tatty T-shirt as best she could and ran a hand through her knotted hair. She wondered what she'd done to make such a good impression. Aveline thought they were still at the *just met* stage.

"Whereabouts do you live?" Aveline asked.

"Oh, in the village, but on the other side. You'll have to come over sometime – we can watch TV and eat mountains of popcorn."

"You don't live in the village itself?" Aveline said, remembering yesterday's pursuit.

"No. Not unless someone moved the house without telling me. Anyway, you must come and visit. It'll be fun."

"That'd be great," Aveline said, excited at the prospect of having another friend to hang out with over the holiday.

"And we can come here together, too," Hazel continued breathlessly. "I love the stones, don't you?"

"Yeah, they're really interesting. I try and imagine what they were like thousands of years ago."

"Much more impressive than they are now, that's for sure. Of course, they were all standing back then. And there used to be a massive circle of wooden stakes surrounding it, so it was like two circles. One made of wood and one made of stone. And there was a huge deep ditch, too. These days they look a little sad."

"Wow, how do you know that?" Aveline asked. Hazel

was becoming more impressive by the second.

"I don't know, I must have read it somewhere," Hazel said, brushing the subject away like a pile of dust. "What's your favourite flavour of ice cream anyway? Mine's triple-chocolate, because you get three times the amount of chocolate for the price of one. What about you?"

"Don't laugh, but I had rhubarb ice cream once in Cornwall and it tasted amazing!"

"Rhubarb? Do you also wear sensible tights and thermals, Grandma Aveline?"

"N-no, I just…" Aveline stammered again, before she saw Hazel grinning. "Oh. Sorry. Yeah, I realize it's odd."

"That's okay, Aveline, it's good to be odd, you know?"

Aveline and Hazel began to explore the stones together, chatting away the whole time, hardly pausing for breath. Hazel peppered her conversation with jokes and random observations about everything and anything, until Aveline's sides ached from laughing so much. Finally, she began to understand why her mum was always on at her to make more friends. Having someone to laugh with felt pretty good. Norton Wick was getting better by the minute.

"I should be heading back soon," Aveline said reluctantly. "My mum's on her own, so I'd best not stay away too long."

"Is your mum a bit strict then?" Hazel said.

"No, she's pretty cool actually," Aveline said, stooping to pluck a dandelion from the grass. "She just likes to know where I am – you know how it is. Her job stresses her out a bit, too. That's why we're here, to relax for a while."

"Well, you couldn't have picked a better place to come," Hazel said, circling one of the stones.

"I know, I think she's enjoying all this fresh air. Makes a change from breathing in exhaust fumes every day."

"No, I didn't mean that," Hazel said, her odd eyes gleaming.

Aveline screwed up her nose. "What do you mean then?"

"I meant you couldn't be staying in a better place than right here." Hazel paused to pat one of the stones. "Next to these."

Aveline took off her glasses and gave them a quick polish. "Yeah, it's cool having them right outside my bedroom window."

"No," Hazel said. "I mean, yes, they're nice to look at, but they're so much more."

"What do you mean?" Aveline asked. Hazel's expression had changed from joking to serious all of a sudden.

44

"It seems I'm going to have to give you another history lesson, Aveline." Leaping up onto the fallen stone, Hazel sat down and crossed her legs. "Let me ask you, what do you think this place is for?"

"Maybe a calendar, possibly a temple, could even be a parking space for UFOs – I don't really know."

"Have you not read *anything* about them?"

Aveline reddened, as if she'd been scolded. She *had* read about them, yes, but it had left her none the wiser really. Plus, Harold had yet to arrive with further research material. Even so, she felt like she must offer something more, if only to prove to Hazel that she was smart too.

"Well, there were so many theories I couldn't decide which one I liked best, though there was something about druids making sacrifices here that sounded scary."

"Oh, the druids were a harmless bunch," Hazel said dismissively. "They wouldn't hurt a fly. But ask yourself why they liked coming here so much. What was it about these stones in particular?"

It was a good question. Aveline had no idea and shrugged her shoulders.

"Because the land that we're standing on is special, Aveline, that's why. I know it looks like a load of old cowpats and nettles, but people have been coming here for thousands of years for good reason. See, everybody thinks that it's the stones that are important, but really they're just fancy markers, like the sign you read when you come into the village. They're simply here to tell people they've arrived at the right place."

Aveline frowned. "The right place for what?"

Widening her eyes, Hazel wiggled her fingertips. "Magic, of course."

A cold breeze brushed against Aveline's bare arms, as if autumn had suddenly decided to make its presence known. The conversation had taken an unexpected turn. Hazel smiled and beckoned Aveline to come and sit beside her, which she did, albeit a little nervously.

"Now, look very closely at my hands," Hazel said, turning them over. "Empty, right?"

Aveline nodded.

Quick as a flash, Hazel clapped her hands together and held them close, before looking Aveline in the eyes and smirking. Then, as if cradling a baby bird, she slowly opened them. In her palm was a necklace: a small silver dolphin pendant attached to a leather strap. Aveline gasped.

"Wow, I love dolphins! They're my favourite."

Hazel reached for Aveline's hand and dropped the necklace into it. "Really? Then you'd better keep this, hadn't you?"

Holding it up, Aveline watched the dolphin swing slowly around on its leather strap, admiring the way it sparkled in the sun's rays. Against the blue sky, it almost looked as if the dolphin was swimming through the ocean. Hazel had performed an impressive magic trick. Aveline had watched magicians on TV but had never seen a trick like this up close. She might have thought Hazel had concealed the necklace up her sleeve, only she didn't have any sleeves. Maybe it had been in the grass, or already on the stone, and she'd picked it up while distracting Aveline when she clapped. Aveline knew enough not to ask how the trick was done. Magicians never revealed their secrets. Sighing, she handed the dolphin necklace back.

"I can't take this. It looks expensive."

Folding her arms, Hazel looked away and raised her chin defiantly in the air.

"Of course you can take it, Aveline. It's nothing to do with me. The stones decided to give you it as a welcome gift. You can't turn it down, it'd be rude."

Aveline glanced around, seeing the stones differently for a second. They almost appeared to have edged closer.

"Are you sure?"

"Quite sure."

Aveline didn't know what to think about that. She'd never been given a gift within five minutes of meeting someone and it put her in a tricky position. She felt like she should refuse it. But she didn't want to hurt Hazel's feelings or look ungrateful. As if sensing her hesitation, Hazel sighed and grabbed Aveline's hand, folding her fingers around the pendant.

"Please, take it. You don't want a horde of angry stones coming after you, do you?"

With a weak smile, Aveline shook her head. "No, I suppose not. Thanks again."

"Don't thank me, thank the stones. Go on, try it on."

Tying it around her neck, Aveline pulled the dolphin up to admire it once more. She noticed that where the dolphin's eye should be, whoever had made it had inserted a tiny blue gem.

"Suits you," Hazel said.

"Thank you, stones," Aveline whispered, before turning back to Hazel. "Want to come and grab a drink at ours?" She wanted to offer Hazel something in return, and with no fancy necklaces to hand, a cold drink would have to do.

"Okay, why not?"

As they walked back across the field, Aveline couldn't help but take another look at her new dolphin necklace. In truth, it felt a little uncanny. She couldn't have picked out a better one herself. It seemed strange, in a way, that Hazel had produced something that was so *exactly* to her tastes. Reaching the back garden of the cottage, Aveline shook the thought from her mind.

"Come on in," she said, giving the gate a kick.

As Hazel walked through into the garden, she suddenly yanked her foot back as if she'd stepped on a hot coal. A grimace of pain flashed across her face and she gritted her teeth.

"Are you alright, did you step on something?" Aveline said, examining the grass for anything sharp.

Hazel's eyes widened and she glanced hurriedly around. "Uh, I...don't know, maybe something stung me."

"My mum will have some ointment for it."

Slipping off her sandal, Hazel rubbed at her foot, her skin pale. "No, it's fine, just gave me a shock."

"Well, at least let me get you something to drink."

Hazel took a backwards step. "Actually, thinking about it, I should probably be getting home."

"Are you sure? It'll only take a minute."

Aveline didn't want Hazel to leave. She wanted to introduce her to her mum. For the conversation to continue. Meanwhile, she noticed that Hazel's mismatched eyes were roving frantically over the garden.

"Bit of a mess in here, isn't it?" Hazel said. "Hard to see where you're stepping, what with all these plants everywhere." Pulling herself up on the garden wall, Hazel peered over it, her eyes narrowing. "Oh, there you are," she muttered. "Nasty little thing." Turning to Aveline, Hazel pointed to the bottom of the wall. "Where did you find *that*, Aveline?"

Looking to where Hazel was pointing, Aveline saw the bottle, just poking its head out of the soil. Hazel must have good eyesight.

"Found it yesterday. I have no idea what's in there." Pulling it out of the soil, she turned and held it towards Hazel. "Have you ever seen anything like this before?"

Holding her hand up, Hazel screwed up her face and backed away.

"Yes, I have. In a dustbin. It's disgusting, Aveline. Looks like someone took a pee in it a few hundred years ago. You should smash it. Like, right now."

Aveline peered into it. "I probably will, but I'm going

to wait and see if I can find out what it is first. My friend, Harold – you'd really like him – well, he's going to search through this bookshop that he works in and…"

Aveline trailed off as she realized she was talking to herself.

Hazel had disappeared.

"Mysterious blaze destroys
Norton Wick home."

The Norton Wick Digest,
September, 2004.

Chapter 4

A Small Sacrifice

Hazel's disappearance had been almost as impressive as her magic trick with the necklace. Aveline had hunted high and low, initially assuming that her new friend must have ducked behind the wall to put her sandal back on or something. But when it became clear she wasn't there, and hadn't nipped down the side of the cottage or back into the field, Aveline had been left feeling distinctly unsettled. That was twice in two days that she'd been given the slip. Had Hazel's foot hurt more than she'd let on and she'd run home? Or had Aveline upset her in some way, maybe said the wrong thing? She hoped not. But for the rest of the day, she couldn't get the strange disappearance out of her mind.

*　　*　　*

The next morning, there came a knock on the door.

"Get that, will you, love?" Aveline's mum shouted from the settee.

"Okay." As she swung the front door open, Aveline was surprised to see Hazel standing outside the gate. She must have knocked and then run back.

"Morning," Hazel called. "Feels like it's going to be another scorcher. What are you up to?"

"What happened to you yesterday?" Aveline said, walking down the path to meet her. "You disappeared into thin air. I would have given you a call, but I don't have your number."

"Oh, I just remembered that I needed to get back. I'd forgotten to do something really urgent and I was in such a panic I didn't have time to tell you. Anyway, I don't have a number, because I don't have a phone."

So Hazel was unusual in more ways than one. Aveline didn't know anyone her age who didn't own a phone.

"Want to come over to the stones again?" Hazel asked, before lowering her voice. "I can show you some more magic if you like."

"Um…okay," Aveline said hesitantly. Yesterday had been fun, but it had also been unsettling when she'd felt almost like Hazel had read her mind. Now Aveline wondered what else Hazel had up her sleeve – or not. "Why don't you come in while I get my shoes on?"

Tentatively, Hazel placed a foot on the path, winced, then drew it back. "Nah, it's alright, I'll meet you over there."

Aveline watched as Hazel turned and strode away, whistling a happy tune as if she didn't have a care in the world. Hazel was unlike any of Aveline's classmates, but Aveline couldn't quite put her finger on why exactly that was. The girl was perfectly ordinary in some ways, extremely puzzling in others.

"Mum, I'm just going over to the stones for a while, is that okay? I'm going to meet that girl I told you about."

Putting down her book, Aveline's mum pulled herself up into a sitting position.

"The one who did a disappearing act?"

"Yep. Her name's Hazel Browne. Brown with an *e*. That was her at the door."

"Okay, just remember that your aunt, Mr Lieberman and Harold are arriving sometime this afternoon. It'd be nice if you were here to greet them."

Aveline hadn't forgotten. It had been the first thing she'd thought about when she'd woken up. To begin with, she'd worried that Harold would be bored here. But with Hazel's arrival and the bottle mystery to solve, not to mention the stones and the necklace trick, she couldn't wait to show him around.

"Don't worry. I won't be long."

"Where did you get that, by the way?" Aveline's mum said, pointing at the dolphin necklace.

"Oh, this?" Aveline tried to appear nonchalant. "Um, Hazel gave it to me yesterday."

"That looks expensive. Bit strange, isn't it, giving necklaces to people you've only just met?"

"Maybe she's just really generous," Aveline said defensively. Even though she'd had the same thought herself, for some reason her mum's comment annoyed her.

"Maybe she is, but all the same, perhaps you should give it back?"

"I tried to, Mum, honestly. About three times. But she wouldn't take it."

"Okay, well, I still don't think you should accept gifts from strangers, but I won't argue if you're set on keeping it. See you in an hour or so then?"

"Yeah. See you soon."

Exiting through the back door, Aveline fought her way

through the overgrown garden and into the field. A gentle breeze played with her hair. A few clouds lingered, but they were breaking apart into white jigsaw pieces to reveal a deep blue sky beyond. Hazel had been right – the temperature was climbing. Pausing, Aveline bent down and turned up the bottoms of her jeans, allowing the air to fan her ankles.

When she raised her head, she saw Alice, the vicar, standing in the centre of the stones. She had her back turned to Aveline and wore the same slightly mismatched outfit as the previous day. Aveline hesitated, unsure if she should announce her presence, as it appeared Alice was in the middle of something.

Something very unusual.

She had her hands raised to the sky, and although the breeze snatched the words away, Aveline could hear Alice murmuring in a strange language. She shrank back as the older woman bent to the ground to pluck a handful of grass, which she threw into the air. Aveline didn't understand what was going on. Why would the local vicar be doing this in the stone circle? And where had Hazel got to? As Aveline wondered what to do, Alice turned and saw her.

"Lovely day for it," Alice called out.

Aveline wasn't sure what *it* was exactly, but nodded in agreement anyway. "Yes…"

"I can see from your expression that you're a little confused."

"No, not at—"

Alice held up a hand. "Fear not, Aveline. I'm simply indulging in some healing work. You pluck a blade of grass, whisper in its ear what you want, then you let it fly away on the breeze. Just a harmless little ritual I picked up."

"Oh," Aveline said. So Hazel wasn't the only one who thought the stones were magic then, though it seemed a strange thing for a vicar to be doing.

"Yes, just doing my bit to put some positive energy out into the world. I think it needs all the help it can get at the moment, don't you? And it's much nicer over here than in the church. That place always feels so cold, even on the hottest days. Did you find your phantom horse-rider by the way?"

It took Aveline a second or two to understand what Alice meant, but then she nodded. "Yes, I did, she lives in the village."

"Oh, really?" Alice's expression seemed to darken a little. "Maybe I was mistaken then – it wouldn't be the first time. Anyway, I must be off. I have a service in an hour, so I'd better get back just in case somebody shows up. You never know, miracles do happen."

Chuckling to herself, Alice threw one last handful of grass into the air and strode away. Aveline frowned. She'd seen vicars holding services in a church before, but never throwing grass around in a stone circle. Once Alice had gone, Aveline called out.

"Hazel! Are you here?"

A magpie swooped low across the field before landing in the long grass, where it glowered at Aveline. Was it the one from the day before? Magpies did all tend to look the same. Sticking out her tongue, Aveline turned away and walked to where Alice had been standing. For a few minutes she examined the ground, but she couldn't see anything which shed further light on "the harmless ritual" she'd just seen.

A tap on her shoulder made her spin around.

"What was *she* doing here?" Hazel said, her eyes glittering.

"The vicar? I don't really know, to be honest. Throwing grass in the air and saying something in a strange language."

"Oh, well that makes perfect sense." Hazel nodded with a grimace.

"It does?" Aveline said, puzzled. She'd never seen anything which made *less* sense.

"Yes, of course. She was here doing her terrible spells."

Cold fingers trailed over Aveline's skin. "What?"

"She's a witch. Everyone in the village knows it, that's why nobody goes to church. They're all afraid of her."

Aveline stared in the direction of the church. She could see its flag waving in the breeze on top of the bell tower. It couldn't have looked more normal.

"Are you sure? I don't think witches are allowed to be vicars."

"Not all witches have green skin and fly around on broomsticks."

"No, I know that, it's just a surprise. Anyway, even if she is a witch, she didn't look like she was doing anything scary when I saw her just now."

"That's because it's daytime. The bad stuff happens at night."

Aveline's stomach lurched. "Really?" Norton Wick suddenly felt a little colder. "Like what?"

"Broken windows. People's things mysteriously disappearing. Missing pets. Twigs snapping in the hedgerows when there's nobody there. More fires than are normal for a village of this size. There's always something."

"And you're saying it's all Alice's fault?" Aveline said, frowning. She didn't quite know what to think about this new information. Norton Wick was just a quiet little village, wasn't it?

"I'm just telling you how it is," Hazel said, adopting an innocent smile. "But you know, magic can be a good thing too. You remember that necklace from yesterday?"

Aveline nodded. "Yes."

"Today I thought we could get you something else."

"Oh, I can't accept any more gifts. It was hard enough explaining to my mum where this came from," Aveline said, holding up the dolphin pendant.

"Don't worry about that," Hazel said breezily. "This is a Witch Stones tradition. It's like a game. Lots of people who come here do it. So…right now, if you could have anything, what would you like?"

Aveline wasn't wholly reassured by Hazel's explanation, but in the spirit of having a good time, she decided to play along.

"I don't know, that's a tough question."

Hazel screwed up her face in disdain. "Really, Aveline? There's nothing at all that you want? I didn't realize you were the girl who had everything."

"No, I'm not, I just don't really need anything right now."

Hazel cast a glance at Aveline's T-shirt and pointed. "What about a replacement for that? Looks like you could do with one."

Aveline looked down, then lifted one arm. Right underneath her armpit there was a big hole. Blushing, Aveline quickly put her arm back down.

"Oops, I didn't notice that. Well, yeah, maybe I could do with a new one."

"Great. So now we know what you want, we just need payment. What have you got?"

Flushing, Aveline pushed back her spectacles. She didn't realize there'd be money involved in this *tradition*, which was something of a sore point, as neither she or her mum had any. It didn't usually bother Aveline, but something about Hazel's stylish jeans and cool camouflage T-shirt made her embarrassed to admit it. Yet Hazel's eyes shone with mischief and excitement. It was impossible to refuse. Digging into her pocket, she pulled out a pile of change.

"Um, I've probably got around two pounds."

Hazel slowly shook her head. "I'm not talking about *money*. See, if you give the stones something that's precious and personal to you, then they'll give you something in return. That's how it's always worked. People used to sacrifice their best goat, or they'd leave their favourite weapon, like a sword or axe or something. Sometimes they'd leave gold or silver. Or just food if that's all they could afford. Even a sack of mouldy oats is precious if you're starving."

"Well, that's all I can afford," Aveline said, pulling out the linings of her pockets for Hazel to see. "Can't see the stones being very happy with that, not if they're used to gold and fancy axes."

"Okay, well, how about that bracelet?" Hazel said, pointing at Aveline's wrist.

Pulling the slim leather band off her wrist, Aveline hesitated. "My mum bought me this though."

"That's exactly what I mean, Aveline. Things like that are much more valuable than money."

"I don't know, I never take this off."

"Come on, it's just a bit of fun – remember, what holidays are for?"

Giggling, Aveline reluctantly placed the bracelet on the stone. It felt like the start of a magician's show, when they ask you to pick a card. While part of her felt nervous, her heart thumped excitedly.

Waving her hand over the bracelet, Hazel closed her eyes and intoned in a deep voice, "Oh, great, wise stones, please accept Aveline's humble offering and send her something nice to replace her tatty T-shirt."

Opening her eyes, she winked at Aveline. "Okay, that's it."

Laughing, Aveline made to reach for her bracelet, but Hazel grasped her by the wrist. Not painfully, but with a forcefulness that made Aveline jump.

"You've got to leave it here, Aveline," Hazel said, in a low voice that carried a faint hint of menace. "Otherwise it won't work."

Aveline was taken aback. She suddenly felt uncomfortable, as if she'd broken some unwritten rule. She thought they'd just been messing around. Hazel's reaction suggested otherwise. "Oh, sorry, I didn't realize."

Hazel released her and smirked. "Those are the rules. If you want the magic to happen then that's the price. Not much to pay for something nice and new though, don't you think?"

Aveline offered a weak smile. "I suppose."

Hazel's eyes locked on her, almost daring her to change

her mind. Aveline didn't feel confident enough to do so, despite the guilt that weighed heavily in her stomach. Her mum would be upset if she noticed the bracelet missing… but Aveline wanted Hazel to like her. Maybe she could pop back later and retrieve it once Hazel had gone.

"Um…do you want to come back to ours?" Aveline said. She wanted to move the conversation on. "My friend's arriving soon. He's staying for a few days. I think you'd like him."

Hazel's eyes narrowed. "You've got a friend coming?"

"Yes, Harold. I think you'd get on."

"Are you sure about that? I'm very picky when it comes to friends, Aveline."

"I'm positive. We can get a drink while we wait, too, it's boiling."

"Will your mum mind?" Hazel said.

"Not at all. And she just happens to be the best home-made lemonade maker in the world."

"You're funny," Hazel said, allowing Aveline to pull her up off the stone. "Okay, let's go. You know, I think you and me are going to get along."

Aveline was glad when she heard Hazel say that. It felt good to make a new friend. Even one who sometimes played very strange games.

"BEWARE THE WITCH STONES!"

Graffiti, 2016. Removed by local council.

Chapter 5
Old Friends

As they walked back up to the cottage, they saw Aveline's mum standing in the back doorway.

"Hello, girls," she called, before making her way down to join them, expertly swatting away the weeds and plants like a gardening ninja.

"That's my mum," Aveline said to Hazel.

They met at the bottom of the garden. Aveline called over the wall. "Mum, this is Hazel."

"Hello, Mrs Jones," Hazel said. "It's lovely to meet you."

"Hello, Hazel. Nice to meet you, too. How were the stones? Did you and Aveline have a good time together?"

"*Mum,*" Aveline said, desperately wanting her to play it cool.

"Yes, we did, Mrs Jones. Are you having a lovely time in Norton Wick?"

As Hazel and her mum chatted, Aveline saw her mum smiling at everything Hazel had to say, nodding along as if she couldn't quite hide her approval. Hazel had obviously made a good first impression. But something niggled Aveline. She couldn't ever remember telling Hazel her surname. So how did she know to call Aveline's mum *Mrs Jones*?

She didn't have a chance to think about it any further, as a car horn sounded from the front of the house.

"Ooh, that'll be our guests!" Aveline's mum said. "Come on, let's go and say hello. Hazel, would you like to come and meet them, too?"

"It's okay, I've got to be going. I don't want to get in the way if Aveline's friend is here."

Aveline didn't know what to think about that. Hazel sounded as if she was jealous, though her wide smile reassured Aveline. If she *was* jealous, she certainly didn't look it.

"Maybe we can meet up tomorrow?" Aveline said, watching her mum eagerly make her way back through the garden.

"Maybe," Hazel said. "If you're not too busy with Harold."

"We can show him the stones?" Aveline suggested.

"Okay," Hazel replied, turning away and walking off through the grass. "Perhaps he'll want to see some magic, too?" she called back over her shoulder.

Which reminded Aveline about the strange ritual they'd just conducted. She was tempted to go and retrieve her bracelet straight away, but she heard her mum calling and ran inside. It'd still be there later; she could go and grab it then.

She couldn't help but feel a surge of excitement as she ran through the cottage and saw Mr Lieberman's old Mini parked out front. Her aunt was at the wheel. Of course – she always liked being in charge. In the passenger seat, Mr Lieberman waved with his bony hand. Harold sat in the back seat and pressed his face and hands against the window, as if he'd just been catapulted into it, his long, almost black fringe plastered against the glass like an ink blot. It appeared he hadn't changed since Aveline saw him last.

Aunt Lilian slid out of the car in one smooth movement and came to give Aveline and her mum a hug. Tall, slim and hard-boned, with her hair pulled back severely and her stiff smile looking like it had been forced into place, it was business as usual for her aunt.

"Hello, my dears, how are you both?" Aunt Lilian said, gathering them in an embrace. For a brief moment, Aveline pressed her face into her aunt's cardigan, savouring the slightly clinical aroma of lavender soap.

"I've missed you," her aunt whispered in her ear.

"Me too," Aveline said.

Mr Lieberman stood politely behind her aunt, trilby hat in hand.

"Ernst, how are you?" Aveline's mum said. "I'm so happy you could all make it. I hope the drive wasn't too long and boring."

"On the contrary, Susan, it was most edifying. I don't get out of Malmouth much these days, you see, what with the bookshop and all, and our route just happened to take us past some very interesting historical sites, including a hill fort that I believe was the site of a major battle in—"

"Ernst," Aunt Lilian said sharply, using Mr Lieberman's first name as shorthand for *shut up*.

"Harold, lovely to see you again, too," Aveline's mum said. "Come on, all of you, let's go inside and I'll give you a tour of the cottage. Though I'm afraid you'll have to reserve judgement, it's definitely seen better days. In fact, best not to lean against anything or the whole place will probably collapse."

Harold lingered behind, sneakily miming a yawn in Aveline's direction.

"I can't tell you how glad I am to get out of that car," he whispered. "Blah, blah, blah non-stop for the last three hours. It was like listening to a broken satnav."

"I bet," Aveline said, hiding her smile with a hand.

"I hope this place is better than Malmouth."

"It's pretty quiet."

"Yeah, I sort of got that impression. Where are those stones you told me about then?"

"You can see them from my bedroom window. They're literally right behind the house."

"Well? Let's go and have a look then. Some tour guide you are."

Usually Aveline would have said something like, *Put a sock in it, Harold.* But his banter made her feel oddly relieved. After her weird last encounter with Hazel, he made everything seem normal again.

Inside, while her mum continued the grand tour, Aveline led Harold through the cottage and up the stairs to her bedroom. All the clouds had dispersed now. The sky and air were clean and crisp, offering a stunning backdrop to the stones. Aveline pushed the window open before glancing at Harold, trying to gauge his reaction.

Harold wasn't normally one for showing his emotions. He tried to play everything cool, as if nothing really impressed him.

"Not bad," he said, true to form. "Hardly Stonehenge though, is it?"

"Yeah, unfortunately there aren't any holiday cottages smack bang in the middle of Stonehenge or we'd be staying there instead."

"I'm not saying they're not cool," Harold replied, flashing her a sheepish smile. "Maybe we can go and have a nose around? We might find a Saxon hoard of gold and become rich and famous."

"Yeah, maybe."

"Anyway, that reminds me, wait here a second. I've brought you something," Harold said, before dashing downstairs. A moment later he reappeared with some books in his arms. "Managed to dig out a few books I think fit the bill. There are a few more in the car, too."

Harold plonked himself down on the floor. After a sneaky glance out of the window, Aveline settled beside him. She had a niggling feeling that out there in the late summer day, a pair of odd-coloured eyes observed her every move. All this talk of magic and witches, together with Hazel's curious tricks, was beginning to make her imagine things. She brought herself back to the present, eager to see what Harold had brought.

"What you got then?" she said.

Ironically, the first book Harold passed her had a picture of Stonehenge on the cover.

"This one's about Neolithic sites in the UK and Ireland. The Norton Wick stones get a mention – here, I've bookmarked it for you," Harold said, pointing to a Post-it note stuck in the top.

Taking a quick flick through, Aveline read the first few lines of the relevant section.

The Norton Wick stone circle is found in the village of Norton Wick in the south-west of England, a few miles outside Bristol. Part of a rich tapestry of similar sites in the area, they're believed to have been constructed sometime around 4000 BC and present an excellent example of a well-preserved Neolithic henge, although the ditch that originally surrounded the stones was filled in sometime during the late Medieval period. Known locally as The

Witch Stones, a recent geophysical survey revealed
the existence of an additional outer ring, constructed
from wooden posts.

Hazel had been right about that then. She must have
read the same book.

"Thanks, Harold."

"Yeah, I know it's a bit dry, but don't worry, there's more
to come," Harold said, pushing across a thinner volume.

Aveline perused the cover.

FOLKLORE AND CUSTOMS OF THE
BRITISH ISLES.

"This one's a bit weird, but it's a good read," Harold
explained. "You wouldn't believe some of the freaky
things people used to do. Anyway, I've stuck bookmarks
in the relevant parts."

Impressed with Harold's thoughtfulness, Aveline
turned to the first section that he'd marked.

There are a number of folklore traditions associated
with the Norton Wick stone circle, most notably the
legend that the circle was created when a coven of

witches was discovered dancing on the Sabbath and turned to stone. However, this tale, or a variation of it, is often found in the context of Neolithic sites, as they were commonly used as cautionary tales to warn people away from the old pagan beliefs.

Aveline thought this was more interesting, though it was a little disappointing that loads of other stone circles in the country had similar legends attached to them. Aveline had been expecting – and hoping for – something a little more…supernatural. But at least she now knew how the stones had got their name. Harold had already come up with the goods. She was about to ask him what else he had when her mum called up the stairs.

"Are you two hiding? Come down and eat something."

Downstairs, Aveline smiled as she saw her mum relishing her role as host. Every five minutes she'd disappear into the kitchen, before reappearing with a plate of something tasty. As usual, Mr Lieberman did most of the talking. Normally, Aveline liked to sit and listen to him, enjoying both his stories and the barely disguised frustration of her aunt, who struggled to hide her impatience. Yet Aveline found it difficult to concentrate and drifted away to her own thoughts.

Which were mostly of Hazel.

She kept remembering how uncomfortable she'd felt at the stones when Hazel had persuaded her to give up her bracelet. And for what? Some nonsense about getting a new T-shirt. She was positive she'd never mentioned her surname, too, so how had Hazel known it? And then there were her accusations that Alice was a witch... Could it be true?

Aveline knew from her own research that there were white witches, who used their magic for good. And Alice hadn't exactly concealed her ritual in the stones. If anything, she'd seemed rather proud of it. Maybe you could be a vicar and a good witch both at the same time? Personally, Aveline couldn't see anything wrong with throwing grass around while trying to make the world a better place. Yet Hazel's description of the creepy and mysterious events within Norton Wick, and her dark hints that Alice was somehow responsible, seemed totally at odds with the eccentric but warm person Aveline had met.

She started as she heard her name being called.

"Aveline, I've brought you a gift I thought you might like. I know it's not your birthday but I just felt the urge to get you something." Aunt Lilian passed a small package towards her. "I have the receipt if you don't like it. It's no problem to take it back and exchange it for something else."

"Is it a portrait of me?" Harold asked, swishing his fringe over his eyes. "You can put it above the fireplace."

"I hope not," Aveline said, excitedly unwrapping the gift.

It only took a moment to pull off the paper. Yet as she saw what it was, a breath caught in Aveline's throat and her stomach churned with an anxiety she didn't quite understand.

Inside lay a brand-new T-shirt.

One that looked identical to Hazel's.

"She is suspected to be a witch & known
to have used sorcery or charms."

Witch Trial, England, 1605.

Chapter 6
Three's A Crowd

For Aveline, the rest of the evening passed in a blur. As she lay on her bed, waiting for her whirling thoughts to slow, she couldn't help but wonder about the arrival of the T-shirt and its mysterious connection to the ritual they'd done. Perhaps Hazel had known in advance that Aveline's aunt would be bringing her a T-shirt. But how on earth could she? Which left another option that Aveline couldn't ignore.

It had been magic.

Real magic.

Aveline had asked for something, left an offering, and the stones had listened.

Which Aveline couldn't quite bring herself to believe.

She considered waking Harold up and asking him what he thought, but the more she thought about it, the more outlandish it seemed. Anyway, she'd heard of people arriving at a party only to discover that they were wearing the same outfit as somebody else, so maybe that's all it was? One big coincidence.

These thoughts continued for some time, until sleep eventually spread itself over her, filled with half-remembered dreams of mysterious girls and standing stones and T-shirts.

The next morning, Harold woke her with a knock on the bedroom door.

"I believe you booked an alarm call?" he said, poking his head through.

Aveline laughed and pointed at his hair, which looked like a very badly made bird's nest. "Looks like someone had a fight with the pillow and lost."

Harold smoothed it down with a hand. "Nothing a quick splash of water won't fix," he said. "Anyway, here's another book I dug out that may prove useful."

"Straight down to business, eh?"

"Yup."

He held the book up for her to see. Reaching for her glasses, Aveline popped them on and squinted across the room.

A Guide to Antique & Vintage Glassware.

"Thought you could show me your famous bottle and we can see if it's in here?"

Over breakfast, Aveline's mum told them that she, Aunt Lilian and Mr Lieberman were going to go for a drive and that they were welcome to come too if they didn't mind hanging out with the oldies for a while. Aveline heard Harold cough and looked up to see him swivelling his eyes while twisting his mouth as if he was chewing on a particularly sticky toffee.

"No need to pull stupid faces, Harold," Aunt Lilian said, casting a withering glance in his direction. "We were only being polite."

"Ach, and please don't get into any mischief while we're gone, Harold," Mr Lieberman interjected. "Trouble and you always seem to have a habit of finding each other."

"Don't worry, Uncle, Aveline will look after me, she never gets in any trouble," Harold replied, rolling his eyes in Aveline's direction. She immediately understood what Harold was getting at – the ghostly experiences they'd shared together in Malmouth. It was one of those occasions where the less said, the better.

With everyone agreeing to meet later on, Aveline took Harold to show him the bottle. She cleaned the soil off as best she could and together they leafed through the pictures in the book, looking for a match. While some examples in there looked similar, they couldn't find one that matched exactly. Aveline twirled the neck of the bottle in her fingers, wondering what to do.

"Like I said before, you should smash it."

They looked up to see Hazel leaning over the garden wall, a pair of yellow-framed sunglasses hiding her eyes.

"Nice T-shirt by the way," she added, nodding at Aveline, who was wearing the new one Aunt Lilian had bought her.

"Um, thanks," Aveline said, the blush on her cheeks having nothing to do with the midday sun. "This is Harold, by the way, who I told you about. Harold, this is Hazel, she lives in Norton Wick."

"Hello, Harold," Hazel said, taking off her glasses to fix him with a very direct stare from her unusually coloured eyes. "I take it you're the smelly-old-bottle expert."

Harold shook his fringe down over his eyes. Aveline noticed he appeared to have suddenly become very shy.

"Er, no, not really, but I did find a book about them. We were just looking to see if we could find a match," he mumbled, holding the book out in front of him like an apology.

"I'll tell you where you'll find a perfect match, Harold," Hazel said, drawing out his name like a strand of chewing gum. "In a landfill site. Now let's get on with it and see what's inside."

Harold looked at Aveline, who shrugged her shoulders. She was desperate to see what it contained. "Okay, let's do it."

It only took a gentle tap against the garden wall to crack the bottle into glassy green fragments. Something fell to the ground as a strong sulphurous smell rankled Aveline's nostrils. Out of the corner of her eye, she saw Hazel shudder, as if summer had just turned to winter. Picking aside the fragments of dirty glass, Aveline bent closer to see what had fallen out.

Tiny black iron nails.

Long, thin and gnarled, like ancient thorns.

Five of them altogether.

They must have caused the rattling sound she'd heard.

There didn't appear to be anything else of significance left in the bottle, just an oily residue on the fragments, and, given the rank odour, Aveline didn't fancy dipping her finger in it.

So that was that.

A bottle with five nails in it.

As she gathered the nails up from the grass, a jolt of electricity passed through her fingertips. She drew back her hand, frowning at them. Maybe she'd brushed against the sharp end of one? Tentatively she touched them again, but while they felt unusually warm, that was all. Cradling them in her hand, she examined them more closely, sensing that she'd missed something important. Why would anyone go to the trouble of squeezing a few nails into a glass bottle before burying it? She held them out for Harold and Hazel to see.

"Can't see you winning Archaeologist of the Year with that," Harold said.

"No," Aveline conceded. "Makes me wonder why someone bothered making the effort. There's got to be a reason."

Swinging her legs over the garden wall, Hazel came

and joined them, peering into the palm of Aveline's hand.

"The reason is that people are weird, Aveline. There's an old woman in the village who collects porcelain frogs. She's got hundreds of them and lines them up in her windows. Must take her hours to dust them all. Why would anyone think that's a good use of their time? Anyway, at least you got to the bottom of it." Hazel stretched out a toe and kicked at a shard of glass. Aveline made a note to come back later and clean it up.

"Should we go over to the stones?" Aveline asked, tucking the nails away into her back pocket. Something told her they might come in useful.

"If you like," Harold said, flicking away his fringe with what appeared to be a quick, nervous glance at Hazel. "I haven't actually seen them up close yet."

"Why not?" Hazel said. "We can show you what they're really all about."

Which Aveline thought sounded a bit like a threat.

As they walked through the field, Harold drifted off to examine one of the few stones that was still standing. While he was out of earshot, Aveline pulled Hazel to one side.

"You noticed it then," Aveline said, stretching out the

bottom of her T-shirt for Hazel to see. "My aunt brought it for me. Bit of a surprise, to say the least. So, I'm a little confused. Does that mean the magic worked?"

"Of course. I told you it would. The stones liked your bracelet, Aveline, that's all. Give and you shall receive. It's just like a shop, only it's magic and it's made of ancient stone and it doesn't close in the evening."

Aveline glanced over to where Harold had bent down in front of one of the stones. He appeared to be trying to poke his fingers into one of the crevices on its gnarled, lichen-covered surface.

"But…the circle's not really magic, is it?" Aveline said. "Things like that don't happen in real life, do they?"

"Yes, they do, Aveline," Hazel said with a dismissive flick of her hand. "Haven't you ever experienced something you can't explain?"

Aveline had no choice but to nod. She had. And she'd never forget it. "But I still don't understand…"

"You don't *need* to understand. All you have to do is accept that it's possible. This place is truly magic, Aveline, it has been for thousands of years. And you've only seen the tip of the iceberg."

They were distracted by the sight of Harold walking towards them, holding out something in his hand.

"What do you think this is?" he said. Between his fingers he held a tiny paper scroll, tied with what appeared to be a strand of cotton.

"Found it wedged into a hole in one of the stones."

"Litterbugs, can't stand them," Hazel said. "Take it home with you, Harold, put it in the bin and that'll be your good deed for the day."

"Not sure it's litter," Harold said. "Somebody's taken care with this, see? They've even rolled it up and tied it so it would fit neatly in the hole."

He slowly unwrapped the tiny scroll, before holding it out for them to see. Despite the heat of the day, a shiver tiptoed across Aveline's skin. There was writing on it. A short message, written in red ink.

"What does it say?" Aveline said, dipping her head for a closer look.

Bring her to me.

Underneath that was a symbol, two vertical lines bisected by one horizontal one.

Aveline suppressed a shudder. Something about the

wording unsettled her. It read like a command. And it made it sound as if whoever *her* was wouldn't have much say in the matter.

"Kind of looks like an H," Harold said, peering at the symbol.

"H for Harold," Hazel said with a sly smirk. "If you're going to write down strange messages and stuff them into the stones, you should at least sign your full name."

With a swift movement she grabbed the paper out of Harold's hand, before ripping it up into tiny pieces and throwing them in the air. "There…and before you call *me* a litterbug, I'd like to remind you both that paper decomposes, so no cows will be hurt."

Harold glanced over at Aveline, his face scrunched in confusion. Aveline felt taken aback, too. They'd found a secret message hidden in a standing stone and Hazel had ripped it up and thrown it away. It seemed such a rude and selfish thing to do, especially as they'd had no time to examine it further.

"I certainly didn't write it," Harold muttered. "I have no idea what *Bring her to me* means anyway."

"Probably asking the stones for a girlfriend, I expect," Hazel said, with a snort.

With her eyes hidden behind her sunglasses, Aveline

couldn't tell for certain if Hazel was joking or not. But she could certainly see the warm flush of pink on Harold's cheeks. Tossing his fringe in annoyance, Harold walked over to another one of the stones, leaving Aveline with a horrible feeling that she'd betrayed him in some way. She wanted to call after him, to try and say something that would perhaps defuse the tension in the air, but she couldn't find the right words fast enough.

The day didn't appear to be going as planned. Aveline had hoped they could spend it all getting to know each other, but Hazel seemed to enjoy aiming sly digs in Harold's direction. Her instincts told her that Hazel wasn't trying to be nasty, just mischievous. Her new friend's sense of humour took a little getting used to – if you hadn't met her before then Aveline could understand how you might get the wrong idea. And one thing she knew about Harold was that while he might pretend to be all cocky and confident, in truth he was just as shy as she was. That was one of the reasons they got along so well. Thankfully a ping on her mobile gave her an excuse to bring their short trip out to an end.

Back soon. Bringing fish and chips! Get some plates out. Mum

95

"We've been summoned," Aveline called across to Harold. "Fish and chips on the way."

Harold brightened up at that. "Excellent!"

"You're leaving already?" Hazel said. "We haven't had time to show Harold any magic yet."

"What's all this about magic?" Harold said.

"Oh, I'll let Aveline fill you in," Hazel said. "Anyway, my parents asked if you'd like to come and stay over tomorrow night, Aveline. You know, like we planned?"

While Aveline remembered Hazel saying something about watching films and eating popcorn sometime, she didn't think they'd made firm plans. Certainly not for an overnight stay. She'd thought it was just the type of casual invitation that people threw out when they were getting along. But now Hazel was making it sound as if she'd gone to a lot of trouble to arrange something. It was an invitation which felt hard to refuse.

"Um, can Harold come too?" Aveline stammered.

"'Fraid not," Hazel said immediately, already walking away into the bright sunshine, her shadow dancing behind her on the long grass. "Girls only. Sorry, Harold, but it's only one evening. I'm sure you'll find something to do. I'll see you tomorrow, Aveline."

And with that she broke into a run. Aveline squinted

after her into the sun, until she had to look away. Tiny black dots danced at the edge of her vision and her head felt muddled, as if she might have spent too long out in the fierce heat without a hat.

"Didn't want to come anyway," Harold muttered. "She's a bit kooky if you ask me."

"I'm sorry about that," Aveline said. "I've got to ask my mum first anyway. I didn't even think we'd organized anything. Maybe I can get Hazel to rearrange it. Anyway, come on, let's go and stuff our faces."

"What did she mean about magic?" Harold said, as they walked back towards the cottage.

Aveline hesitated. There wasn't any reason *not* to tell him. She nearly had the night before. Even so, something made her pause, almost as if this was a situation she didn't want to draw Harold into. Yet nor did she want him to feel like she was shutting him out, especially after what had happened earlier with Hazel's sniping. Aveline decided to share what had happened so far: about Hazel's magic trick with the necklace, about Alice the *reputed* witch, and finally about her new T-shirt being conjured up by the stones in exchange for a leather bracelet. When she heard herself talking about it out loud, it all seemed a little ridiculous.

"Hmm, that is strange," Harold said, pushing open the gate to the cottage. "And the T-shirt thing is hard to explain. Did she specifically say, *Bring Aveline the same T-shirt as me?*"

Aveline stopped and grabbed him by the arm. His skin felt warm to the touch after being in the sun all afternoon, and when she released him she saw white marks where her fingers had gripped him. "Harold, you're right. Hazel saw that mine had holes in it, but all she actually said was *something nice*. Still, pretty big coincidence, don't you think?"

"For sure," Harold said. "But probably not magic, eh? Aunts bring nieces presents. Hazel's probably just good at card tricks and educated guesses. Anyway, rather you than me. I wouldn't want to spend the night over at someone's house if I'd only just met them. She might stick you up in the attic and keep you there for ever."

It was only a joke. But what Harold said unsettled Aveline a little. And even the prospect of fish and chips couldn't shake the feeling that she didn't quite know what she'd let herself in for.

"The druids are in charge of all religious matters, superintending public and private sacrifices, and explaining superstitions."

The Gallic Wars
(Commentarii de Bello Gallico),
Julius Caesar, 54BC.

Chapter 7

Bumps in the Night

The fish and chips were hot, salty and greasy, just as Aveline and Harold liked them. Afterwards, as they watched TV with full stomachs, Aveline felt happier than she had been earlier. It was fun having Harold here.

Later that evening, just before bed, they had another look at the pile of books he'd brought with him, which seemed to have grown since Aveline had last seen it.

"I was only joking about bringing the whole bookshop," Aveline said with a smirk.

"Well, I didn't have much time to get organized, so I just grabbed anything that looked like it might fit the bill." Plonking himself down on the floor beside her, Harold swept his fringe out of his eyes, which immediately fell back into the exact same position. "But you know that book I showed you earlier, *Folklore and Customs of the British Isles*?"

"Yeah, it had a section about the stones in it."

"That's right, but have you read the rest of it yet?" Pulling the book onto his lap, Harold turned to a section he'd marked. "Here, look, there's a bit at the end about the village itself you might want to take a look at."

Intrigued, Aveline peered down at where Harold had pressed his finger.

The village of Norton Wick has a long association with witchcraft, dating back to the early 1600s when it was the scene of a notorious witch trial. However, it's further claimed by some historians that the name of the village itself points to an ancient and well-established tradition of pagan practices in the area, with the name Wick said to derive from the Old English word wicca, or <u>wicce</u>, meaning witch.

"Hazel keeps talking about magic, doesn't she?" Harold said with raised eyebrows. "And she says the vicar is a witch, too? Maybe the tradition is still going strong?"

"Oh my," Aveline said, her thoughts immediately

turning to Alice. At that moment, a cold breeze blew in through the window. The fine hairs on her forearms rose up and she smoothed them down with her fingers.

"I'd keep a close eye on both of them if I was you," Harold said, reaching for another book. "Okay, so here's one about druids."

"Wow, you remembered everything."

The picture on the front showed a man in white robes, his hands raised to the sky. Not too dissimilar to the pub sign, only not quite so menacing. This druid looked a bit like Gandalf.

"This one's a little wordy," Harold said. "I've only skim-read it."

"What's it say?"

"Oh, it seems druids are a bit of a mystery alright. Mainly because they never wrote anything down, so we don't have any records. But the author says they were probably like leaders, priests, judges and doctors all rolled into one. Very wise. I think I probably would have been one."

"No, I think you would have been the tribal dung-spreader."

"And you would have been my assistant," Harold said, between snorts of laughter. "Anyway, you haven't seen the best bit yet." He reached over to retrieve yet another book. "I read a little of this just now and I think it might remind you of something."

Harold passed the slim volume over. It had become like a game of pass-the-parcel, only each time a new book ended up in Aveline's lap, it felt as if she was unwrapping another layer of mystery. Angling the spine, Aveline read the title.

MEDIEVAL SUPERSTITIONS AND CHARMS.

Turning to the page with the sticky yellow tab on it, Aveline quickly read what it said.

Superstitions surrounding witches and witchcraft were a part of everyday life in medieval England and, as a result, many charms were developed in an effort to keep both householders and houses safe against evil influences. One notable example is the witch bottle, an early description of which appears in Joseph Glanvill's Witches and Apparitions:
"To protect thyself against the witch's curse, take their Hair, and Cork it in a Bottle with Nails, Pins and Needles, and bury it in the Earth; and that will do the feat."

As Aveline finished the section, she let out a long breath.

"Now, correct me if I'm wrong," Harold said quietly, "but that sounds very much like the bottle you discovered in the back garden – you know, the one we smashed."

"It…does, yeah," Aveline said, her heart fluttering. The description matched precisely. She'd wondered why somebody would go to the trouble of burying a bottle full of nails. Now she had her answer. "But if someone put it there to protect a house against witchcraft…"

"Then we'd better watch out because we're not protected any longer," Harold said. "And with that comforting thought fresh in our minds, I suppose we'd better get to bed."

Before going to bed, Aveline closed the window and locked it, even though it was another warm evening. The thought of the house lying defenceless without the witch bottle wasn't a nice one, but at least locks on windows offered a more solid form of protection. With these unsettling thoughts in mind, sleep was hard to come by. And even when it did finally come, it wasn't to be for long.

At first she thought it was thunder. They'd had a storm

the first night they arrived, the humidity breaking out into daggers of blue light and a brief but heavy deluge. But as she craned her neck to listen, the sound she could hear felt unusually rhythmic.

Thump. Thump. Thump.

It sounded like footsteps, only they were coming from the roof. She debated waking Harold, or her mum, but forced herself to listen a while longer and think of what it could be. A bird? Some kind of nocturnal animal? Did foxes or badgers climb onto the roofs of houses? Probably not. Maybe it was just a squirrel, out having a night-time ramble. Gently pulling back the sheet, Aveline crept to the window and peered out. The moon shone brightly, making everything appear as if it was made of molten silver, the stones like steel blades pointing up into the clear night sky. Pushing open the window as far as it would go, Aveline leaned out and turned, trying to see up onto the roof.

She started as something flew into the air.

A raggedy shape, like a piece of black cloth blown from a washing line.

A bird.

It's only a bird, Aveline told herself, hurriedly blowing out the breath she'd just inhaled.

Closing the window behind her, she locked it, checked it and tiptoed back to bed.

When Aveline awoke, her bedroom felt like a sauna. Popping on her glasses and glancing at her phone, she saw that it was still early. Climbing out of bed, she opened the window and let the air cool her flushed skin. In the pale early morning light, her thoughts were no longer quite so dark. Even those uncanny thumps had a perfectly logical explanation. They were out here in the countryside and the noises at night were different to those in the city, that was all. She would just have to get used to it. But as she made her way downstairs for a glass of orange juice, she noticed something unusual on the doormat – a perfect white square of paper. A letter. Bending down, she saw that it had her name written on it.

Aveline.

The writing was beautiful and looked as if someone had used an old-fashioned ink pen. She didn't get many personally addressed letters. In fact, apart from birthday cards, this was possibly the first one she'd ever received. Strange, too, considering she was only here on holiday.

Hesitantly, she picked it up, opened it, and read what was written inside.

Meet me at 7 tonight, at the bench on the village green. Got something cool to show you. We can go to mine afterwards. Bring your toothbrush. My parents can't wait to meet you! Hazel Browne (with an e)

Upstairs, Aveline could hear doors opening, footsteps thumping, toilets flushing and taps running. It sounded like everybody else was getting up, too. She considered going to show Harold the note, but then decided against it, tucking it inside her pyjamas for safekeeping. Harold already thought Hazel was *kooky*. A personally addressed letter delivered at some strange hour of the night wouldn't help matters. Everyone they knew would have just sent a text. And despite their somewhat frosty first encounter, Aveline desperately wanted Harold and Hazel to get along. Harold was an old friend. Hazel was a new one. And they actually had quite a lot in common. A sense of humour, for one thing. Anyway, Aveline still hadn't decided if she would go to Hazel's house yet. She still had to get permission, plus she didn't want Harold to think she was shutting him out of things just after he'd arrived. She didn't like herself for not telling Harold about the note, but convinced herself that it was for good reason. She didn't want to play piggy-in-the-middle for the rest of the holiday and didn't see why, with a little time, they all couldn't get along just fine.

After they'd finished breakfast, it was the oldies' turn to go and have a look at the stones. Aveline's mum explained to Mr Lieberman and Aunt Lilian how Aveline had become a little obsessed by them and so they should all go and see what they were missing out on.

"It's like living in the middle of prehistory itself," Mr Lieberman said, putting on his trilby hat. "Ach, imagine that, we'll be walking in the exact location where once, ancient architects and builders considered the mighty task before them, mopping their brows while—"

"Ernst, come on, let's go, or we won't be back in time for lunch," Aunt Lilian said, unable to conceal her impatience.

Aveline and Harold chose to stay behind and go for a walk through the village, before they met the rest of them back at the cottage. While they were out, Aveline finally decided that she would go to Hazel's after all, as long as her mum agreed. She couldn't resist seeing where Hazel lived and it would give her a chance to ask some more about Alice – and also if she knew anything about the witch trial.

And so, after lunch, while they had a moment alone, she told her mum about Hazel's offer.

"She's invited me over tonight. Her parents said it would be okay," Aveline said, already knowing – and dreading – what her mum was going to say.

"Of course you can stay at Hazel's tonight, though I'll need to double-check with her parents. Do you have a phone number for them?"

"No, Hazel doesn't have a phone."

"Really? That's unusual. I'm afraid you can't go if I'm unable to speak to them first. Anyway, don't you think it's a little unfair on Harold? He's come all this way just to see you, and he's only here for a few days."

"Yeah, I know," Aveline said, kneading her fingers into knots. "But she sort of put me on the spot. I did ask if Harold could come but she said it was girls only. It's just for one night, Harold will be fine."

Even as she said it, Aveline realized that she sounded exactly like Hazel had yesterday.

"Well, you'll need to find out their phone number or you'll have to unarrange it, I'm afraid."

At that moment, Aveline heard the muffled sound of a phone ringing.

"Is that mine?" Aveline's mum said.

"I think so, Mum, sounds like it's in your handbag."

After a moment's rummaging, her mum found her phone and answered it.

"Hello?" After a brief pause, she said it again. "Hello?"

Aveline's mum frowned, before fiddling with the volume.

"I can't quite...oh hello...yes, this is Susan Jones. I'm sorry? This line is very bad for some reason...yes...yes... oh, hello there...okay...yes...well, that's fine then. And the address?" Scrabbling for a pen, Aveline's mum hastily wrote something down. "Yes...okay...well, thank you for calling. By the way, how did you get hold of my...oh. They've hung up."

Slowly, Aveline's mum placed her phone back in her handbag, staring at it with a puzzled expression.

"Well, Hazel's ears must have been burning. That was her mum, though I couldn't hear her very well. I wonder how she got my number?"

"What did she say?" Aveline asked.

"The gist of it appeared to be that it's okay for you to go and stay over. So fine, you can go, I hope it's fun, but you'll need to make it up to Harold."

"I will, I promise," Aveline said, relieved that she'd been given permission to go, yet suddenly beset by a queasy feeling in her stomach at the thought of spending time with someone she didn't know that well. Meeting people's parents was always nerve-wracking. What if they didn't like her? If only Harold could have come too, she would have been much more relaxed about the whole thing.

For the rest of that afternoon, Aveline did her best to make good on the promise she'd made to her mum. She made Harold and herself milkshakes. Later, Harold wanted to go and have another look at the stones to see if he could find any more notes, and so they went exploring for a couple of hours. They made a complete sweep of the circle and investigated all the nooks and crannies, but didn't stumble upon anything else unusual.

After dinner, Aveline realized it was time to go. She still felt nervous even though she was only going for a sleepover. Yet she'd known Hazel for such a short time. It felt as if this had come a little too early in their friendship. Aveline was also annoyed with herself for having been pulled into Hazel's plans so easily. In hindsight, she hadn't really had much of a say in the matter and she promised herself that Harold would come first for the remainder of the time he was here. She even considered backtracking and making an excuse, until she realized that she had absolutely no idea how to contact Hazel and didn't want to leave her waiting on the village green.

So, after packing her overnight bag, Aveline said her farewells. She noted that Aunt Lilian gave her a very pointed look and knew that her aunt was thinking the same thing as her mum.

Harold walked her to the door. If he was feeling left out, then he wasn't showing it.

"Have a good time at Hazel's. Don't worry about me, I'm really looking forward to watching *Downton Abbey* all night with this lot."

"Thanks," Aveline said with a smirk. "See you in the morning."

"If she offers to show you the attic, just say no."

"Very funny."

Hazel wasn't there when Aveline arrived, so she parked herself on the bench to wait. Admiring her dolphin pendant, Aveline wondered what the night would bring. Despite her nerves, she couldn't wait to see where Hazel lived. Maybe they would go to see the horse, too, and she could feed it an apple and nuzzle its soft, velvety nose.

A tap on her shoulder made her jump.

Hazel sat down beside her, eyes bright like the midday sun. "Hello there, Aveline with an A."

"Hazel, you made me jump," Aveline said.

"Sorry I'm late, I lost track of the time. I was busy getting everything ready for tonight. You excited?"

"Uh, yeah," Aveline said. "But you said you wanted to show me something before we head over to yours?"

"Yes, I do. Come on, we can cut through the village."

"Did your parents really say they wanted to meet me?" Aveline asked shyly, shouldering her bag.

"Oh, they're actually away tonight," Hazel said. "It'll just be me and you."

With that, Hazel scampered off. Despite the residual warmth of the day, Aveline shivered. No parents? That was highly unusual, particularly considering the phone call her mum had received. With trembling hands, Aveline pulled her jacket tight around her shoulders. Now she really wished she'd stayed at home.

"While researching the history of the church
I made a most curious discovery in
the graveyard…"

*Reverend Alexander Robertson, Rector of
St Michael's, Norton Wick 1863–78.*

Chapter 8
A Grave Discovery

The sinking sun pinned long black shadows to the houses. In the amber dusk, a bat swooped past in a feeding frenzy. Aveline normally enjoyed this time of the day, when the light became strangely luminous and everything seemed at peace, but tonight the bats appeared to be fluttering in her stomach, too. Up above a pale waxing moon inched shyly into view. Aveline quickened her step, not wanting to lose sight of Hazel, who ran ahead with her thin summer jacket flapping behind her like butterfly wings.

"Keep up, Aveline, I think you'll like this," Hazel called back, her voice thick with mischief.

As they headed along the lane, St Michael's, the parish church, came into view, its squat tower silhouetted against the reddening sky. Aveline couldn't shake the tingling sensation in her body that told her she might be a little out of her depth.

"What are we doing?" she whispered, following Hazel through the wooden lychgate that marked the entrance to the churchyard. She couldn't see anybody else around, but it still seemed appropriate to lower her voice. She'd heard somebody say once that the dead were just sleeping. Although she now knew that they hadn't meant *literally* sleeping, the phrase had always stayed with her. She really hoped they weren't about to get into trouble. She'd told her mum they were going for a sleepover, not creeping around the local graveyard.

"I'm going to show you a very special grave," Hazel said, her eyes glittering darkly.

"Whose?" Aveline replied.

"The witches'," Hazel said quietly. "The ones who gave the stones their name. The ones they put on trial. Nobody knows where it is – except me."

Aveline already had an answer to one of her questions – it appeared that Hazel *did* know about the witch trial. Once again, it seemed like Hazel could read her mind. So there was more than one witch put on trial? Hazel had definitely said *the ones*…

As Hazel weaved ahead through the gravestones, Aveline tried to keep up, taking care not to step on any of the graves that looked recent or had fresh flowers on them. She glanced up from her tiptoeing just in time to see Hazel disappear around the back of the church. Sighing, she followed. It felt like trying to keep up with a puff of smoke.

The fading sunlight didn't reach this side of the church, and Aveline found herself momentarily disorientated, like she'd walked into a dark room without checking where the light switch was. Hazel stood at the rear of the church, staring at a thin strip of grass. Aveline moved to join her, wondering what the witches' grave would look like.

Only there was nothing to be seen.

Hazel seemed lost in thought. For a second, she raised a finger to her eye. It looked to Aveline like she wiped away a tear.

"Are you okay?" Aveline asked tentatively.

Turning, Hazel flashed her a quick glint of white teeth. "Yes, I'm fine."

"I can't see any graves," Aveline said.

"That doesn't mean there aren't any," Hazel replied.

Her furtive response prompted Aveline to give the narrow strip of grass a second inspection. There weren't any noticeable bumps or lumps in the ground. No hidden gravestones or markers. It resembled a putting green on a golf course.

"But surely if witches were buried here there'd be a gravestone or something?"

"Not if they wanted everyone to forget all about you."

Aveline didn't have time to wonder what Hazel meant by this.

At that moment, a side door opened in the church. A voice called out.

"Who's that out there? I have a heavy candlestick in my hand and we all know what happened to Professor Plum in the library."

Recognizing Alice's voice, Aveline called back.

"Um, it's only me, Aveline. We met in the stone circle the other day. I'm here with my friend."

But as Aveline glanced back to where Hazel had been standing, she realized the girl was nowhere to be seen. Shocked, Aveline whirled around, but the graveyard was quiet and empty. Hazel had done yet another disappearing trick. No sound of footsteps running off into the night. No word of warning. It almost felt unnatural, as if Hazel had pulled on a cloak that made her invisible. A quick flicker of anger warmed Aveline's face. Weren't friends supposed to stick together? Now she had to deal with this alone, and she hadn't forgotten what Hazel had said about Alice being a witch.

Alice stepped out, jamming her bowler hat on her head like the top slice of a sandwich. This evening she'd matched her heavy boots with some lime green socks. Aveline relaxed a little. Alice wasn't scary in the slightest.

"I only see one of you," Alice said. "Did I scare your friend away? I was only joking about the candlestick."

"Um, yeah, I think maybe she got spooked," Aveline mumbled, the flush of anger changing to an equally warm shade of embarrassment.

Alice glanced around the graveyard, her bottom lip sticking out.

"And is this…friend…the same girl you saw riding a horse?"

"Yes, that's her. I don't know where she went, but we're on our way to her house."

"Mmm, interesting. And where does she live exactly?" Alice had the look of a bloodhound that had just caught a scent.

"I've not been there before, but my mum has her address if you need it?"

"No, it's fine, as long as your mum knows where you are," Alice muttered, before glancing at her wristwatch.

"Excuse me for asking, Aveline, but why exactly are you down here at the back of the church? Generally speaking, the only visitors we get down this end are those who are looking to pinch the lead off the roof."

Aveline hesitated, wondering if she should tell the truth. It sounded stupid to say they were looking for a witch's grave. Especially considering what Hazel had told her about Alice.

"We were just reading the gravestones," Aveline said.

Alice's eyes twinkled in the gloom. "Well, you've passed all the graves already."

"Isn't there anybody buried *here* then?" Aveline asked innocently.

Alice stared at her with a curious expression, as if Aveline had just revealed something about herself.

"Why ever would you think that?"

"Oh, it was just something my friend said, about there being unmarked graves here."

"Of course. Your disappearing friend. And in the spirit of being honest, she's correct, though I must say, there aren't many people who are privy to that information."

"She knows a lot about the history of Norton Wick," Aveline said, with more than a hint of pride in her voice.

Alice gave her another pointed look. "Yes, I fancy she

does. Well, as you saw, the official graves are all back that way, on the east and west sides of the church. People weren't generally buried around this side because people used to associate the north with darkness. Anyone placed here would never get to feel the sun's rays, you see, so they would only put people here who they wished to punish. And you know, it's true, it always feels gloomy here, even in the daytime."

"So there is someone buried here then?"

"There are certainly no *official records* of any burials, but back then people were very superstitious – and they could also be very unforgiving. So if somebody committed a crime, or there was simply someone they considered a bad sort, then it wasn't unusual for those people to be buried here, on the north side. For example, people such as…witches."

Funny how the word *witches* kept coming up in Norton Wick, Aveline thought. The gloom seemed to thicken. She didn't quite know what to say. She sensed Alice was toying with her in some way and couldn't tell if it was being done in fun or with a view to discovering what she knew.

"Um, that's so interesting, thanks. I'd better go find my friend now. Sorry again for disturbing you," Aveline said, wanting to escape Alice's probing gaze. All this talk of witchcraft had started to make her nerves feel even more frayed than they did already.

"That's quite alright, Aveline."

As Aveline made to go, Alice touched her on the arm.

"You know, Aveline, you seem like a sensible girl. Don't go getting yourself into any mischief or letting anyone lead you astray. And if you need advice, come and see me, I'm always here."

Frowning, Aveline tried to read Alice's expression. It was such a strange thing to say. Was she warning her about Hazel?

"Um…should I be worried?" Aveline said.

"No, no, just listen to your intuition, is all I'm saying. If something feels wrong, that's probably because it is."

"Okay…um…thanks," Aveline said, unsure what else to say.

"Oh, and take some of this with you," Alice said, reaching into her pocket and pulling out a bunch of herbs. "It's a fragrant little bunch I put together myself – to protect you from negative energies."

"Thanks again," Aveline said, holding the pale leaves up to her nose. "Smells nice."

"Doesn't it just? If you ever find yourself in a situation or place where things don't feel healthy, simply burn it and waft it around. It's a very powerful antidote to bad vibes. Good evening then, and God bless."

"See you."

Pushing the herbs into her pocket, Aveline tightened the straps on her rucksack and headed out of the graveyard, darting glances left and right, trying to see where Hazel had hidden herself. It wasn't until she'd walked through the lychgate that she felt confident enough to call out.

"Hazel?" she shouted despairingly. "Where are you?"

She waited for a reply, feeling fed up. What would she do if Hazel didn't appear? While her mum had the address, Aveline didn't, and if she had to go back to the holiday cottage there'd be a lot of explaining to do. Worse, Harold would never let her hear the end of it. He'd probably start referring to it as *the sleepover where nobody actually slept over*.

For a while she stood alone in the creeping dusk. A sheep bleated somewhere on a hillside, sounding lost and lonely. A narrow band of gold lay on the horizon, but up above the sky had darkened to an inky blue, and the first stars twinkled a welcome.

"What were you talking to *her* about all this time?" said a voice that sounded as cold as midnight.

Aveline spun around. Hazel stood in front of the hedgerow, her eyes glowing like tiny candles.

"Who?"

"*Her* in the church, of course – the witch!"

"I had to explain what I was doing there because *you* left me. Where did you go?"

"I heard her opening the door and scarpered. I thought you'd follow me."

"I didn't even notice you were gone!"

"You'll have to be quicker next time then. Anyway, let's go, we're wasting valuable snacking time."

Hazel set off, walking briskly through a break in the hedgerow and out onto a narrow path that led away from the village. Aveline followed, albeit a little reluctantly.

Hazel hadn't even apologized for leaving her alone at the church. If anything, she'd made it sound like it was all Aveline's fault. Everything Hazel did or said felt slightly peculiar, as if she was living in a different reality to the one Aveline inhabited. There didn't seem to be any shyness or anxiety or regret. Just fearlessness and utter confidence in everything she did. Or at least that's how she came across. Maybe it was all an act?

Aveline hoped she'd know Hazel better by morning. She reached into her pocket to clutch the herbs Alice had given her – something solid to hold onto during a night when everything had begun to feel eerie and uncertain.

They climbed over stiles, wandered up back roads and cut across fields, their footsteps silenced by the thick grass.

"Are we getting closer?" Aveline asked.

"Nearly there," Hazel called back – but that wasn't strictly true as they kept on walking for what seemed like ages. Soon, Aveline was out of breath and had completely lost her bearings. Just as she began to feel like the journey would never end, they reached the brow of a hill and Hazel pointed down into a valley, at the bottom of which lay a small copse of trees.

"There, that's where I live," Hazel said. "Come on."

Aveline followed, intrigued to finally see Hazel's house, though she couldn't see any lights. There didn't appear to be a driveway, or even a road leading up to the house, though it was hard to see anything in the twilight. Maybe Hazel lived in a yurt or a caravan? Something about her suggested she hadn't had a traditional upbringing.

Hazel disappeared between the trees.

Aveline trotted to keep up, tripping over a branch and nearly falling flat on her face. When she clambered to her feet, light suddenly flooded through the trees and Aveline saw that her guess about Hazel living in a caravan couldn't have been more wrong.

"Take a tooth out of a dead man's skull,
and hange the same about the partie's neck,
till the payne cease."

Charm against toothache, The Book of
Magical Charms, *17th century*.

Chapter 9
Hazel's House

Aveline felt a mixture of envy, wonder and delight. Her friend Hazel, it transpired, lived in a millionaire's house.

The walls were all made of glass – huge great windows that slanted at curious angles, lending the place a futuristic appearance. To enhance the effect, the exterior had been lit with spotlights, making it look like the house had been built from crystal. It felt like something from a science-fiction novel about people living on Mars. Hazel beckoned her towards it.

"What do you think?"

"Wow," was all Aveline could say. It was all that needed to be said.

"You like it? Wait until you see inside."

What appeared to be one giant window turned out to have a door concealed within it, which slid open without so much as a squeak. As Aveline walked in, she could smell an exotic aroma of smoky incense. She slid her Dr. Martens off, not wanting to tread muck over the shiny hardwood floors or the expensive rugs.

"This is the kitchen," Hazel said, pointing to the gleaming marble surfaces. "You hungry?"

Aveline grinned. She was always hungry.

Hazel pulled open a black fridge, which Aveline wouldn't have noticed because it blended in so seamlessly with everything else.

"Take your pick," Hazel said.

Aveline could barely believe her eyes. Crammed with cheesecakes, crumbles, cookies, cakes and milkshakes, it felt as if the fridge contained everything she always dreamed about eating. In fact, it was a little strange. She couldn't see a single vegetable in there. No meat or pasta or microwave meals. Hazel flicked open the freezer cabinet, which held at least ten different tubs of ice cream. Right at the front sat a tub of rhubarb flavour.

"I got some especially," Hazel said. "Grab a bowl and help yourself, we'll take it through to the TV room."

Five minutes later, Aveline had a huge bowl of ice cream in one hand and a slice of cheesecake in another, balanced on top of a glass of chocolate milkshake.

They walked through what appeared to be a lounge, with a glass table, cool canary-yellow designer chairs and modern art on the walls. At the end, steps led down into another room. Here, one wall was covered by the largest TV screen Aveline had ever seen. Speakers and mood lighting had been skilfully incorporated into the ceiling. A large comfortable zebra-print sofa invited them to come and relax.

Sinking into the sofa, Aveline placed her sweet treats next to her while Hazel flicked on the TV.

"Where does the horse live?" Aveline asked.

"We stable him at a local farm. Easier that way. Anyway, what do you want to watch? I've got every channel."

"What is it your parents do again?" Aveline asked, gazing around while failing to hide her admiration. It felt like she'd stepped into a glossy magazine.

"Something to do with banking. I don't really understand it, to be honest."

"Oh. Where've they gone tonight?"

"Out with some friends, staying at a fancy hotel in Bristol somewhere."

"Do you think they'd mind me staying over?"

"No, I told them you would be, they said it was fine. Any more questions?"

The way Hazel raised her voice slightly suggested that Aveline should stop using hers. But she was a little nervous. If her mum had known they'd be on their own, she'd never have let her come. Aveline had never spent the night at someone's house without any parents and it wasn't quite as liberating as she'd expected it to be. What if something happened, or one of them had an accident – what would they do?

Trying to relax, Aveline settled back into the sofa as the film Hazel had picked started. She dug out a huge spoonful of ice cream and let its icy sweetness slowly dissolve on her tongue. Despite her misgivings, in some ways it felt like she'd won the lottery. Here was a friend who made her laugh – some of the time, at least – and lived in the fanciest of fancy houses with a seemingly unlimited supply of sweet treats.

And yet.

The house had an eerie atmosphere. It felt empty, without any signs of family life. So far, Aveline hadn't seen a single picture of Hazel with her parents. It could have just been that they didn't want stuff cluttering up the walls of their designer house, but Aveline had never been in a home that didn't have at least a few photos. As she glanced across at Hazel, a slow smile spread across her new friend's face.

"Good here, isn't it?" Hazel said, licking the back of her spoon. "Wouldn't you like to stay for ever?"

"Um, yeah," Aveline mumbled, not sure if she actually would now the novelty was quickly wearing off. Taking a bite of cheesecake, she turned her attention back to the superhero movie they were watching. In truth, while this felt like it should be an experience to savour, the longer she stayed, the more unsettling it became. She knew next to nothing about Hazel or her family, and yet here she was, staying overnight. She actually considered pretending that her mum had texted to say she had to go home, but that would mean walking back to the cottage at night, and that wasn't an option. Not alone through those dark fields. And certainly not in a village where witches were said to dwell.

Halfway through the film, Hazel got up, saying she had to go and prepare the spare bedroom.

Once she'd left, Aveline waited a minute before quietly getting to her feet. Tiptoeing out into the hallway, she tried the handle on the first closed door she came across. It opened, revealing a large, square room. Only it was completely empty. Just bare floorboards and a window. Closing the door as quietly as she could, she crept into the next room along. This one at least had a desk and a chair, but scant else that suggested anything actually happened in there. She still hadn't seen a single photograph, no coats left discarded on the back of a chair, no books or magazines, nor a single pair of broken-in slippers – nothing that suggested any kind of day-to-day routine. Either Hazel's family hadn't been living in the house for long, which at least would account for its sparse appearance, or they simply had more space than they knew what to do with.

"Got bored of the film, did you?"

Aveline started. Once again, she hadn't heard Hazel approach.

"I was just looking for the loo," Aveline said, glad that she'd thought of an excuse beforehand. This was fast becoming a truly uncomfortable experience. Not for the first time, Aveline wished she hadn't been so quick to accept Hazel's invitation.

After they returned to the TV room, Hazel suggested another film, but Aveline felt too unsettled. There were just the two of them in this big house. They hardly knew each other. It all felt too much, too soon.

"I don't think so. I have to get up early tomorrow and walk back across to the cottage."

"Suit yourself. You can come here anytime. Every day if you like. Come on, I'll show you where we're sleeping."

They passed through some more painfully stylish rooms, which seemed to have no purpose other than to look good, before Hazel led her up a winding stairway to the upper level.

"Here you go," Hazel said, opening a cream door. "It has a whirlpool bath if you fancy a dip before bed."

"Wow!" Aveline gasped. "This is amazing!" The bedroom looked bigger than the entire cottage where they were staying. Everything had been furnished in bright pastel colours, from the bedspread and curtains down to the thick, soft carpet. There were beanbags and games consoles. The walk-in closets were huge with full-length mirrors inside, and there was a suitably gigantic bed.

"Plenty of room for us both," Hazel said.

Aveline fetched her toothbrush and wandered into the bathroom to clean her teeth. Its chrome fittings sparkled. The matching towels and bathrobes were soft to the touch. There were lotions, soaps and scrubs made from coconut and peppermint. In the wide, spotless mirror, Aveline made a foamy white grimace at herself before spitting down the plughole. Once done, she pulled the blind up and peered out of the window. The moonlight illuminated a well-kept lawn. Beyond that lay the thick ring of trees they'd walked through to get here. Maybe Hazel's parents had planted them like that to give themselves some privacy, Aveline thought, though it wasn't really necessary. They appeared to be well outside the village with no close neighbours.

The temperature was beginning to drop at night now summer had nearly come to an end. She could feel the cold trying to reach out to her from beyond the glass. Picking up her phone, she started typing a text to her mum, only to realize there wasn't any signal. No surprise, really, considering the remote location, yet it made her feel unpleasantly alone. Shivering, she changed into her pyjamas and returned to the bedroom.

Hazel was already in bed. Climbing in next to her felt a bit awkward. Aveline had expected to have her own room, especially in a house this size. Hazel insisted on brushing Aveline's hair, before pulling off her own hairbands and using them to tie Aveline's hair into bunches, which made them both giggle.

As they chatted, Aveline began to feel more relaxed.

"Okay, how about this?" Hazel said, her eyes shining. "You tell me a secret about yourself and I'll tell you one about me."

Aveline didn't really want to divulge anything secret about herself but saw it as a good opportunity to learn more about Hazel so she gave it some thought.

"Okay, well...um," Aveline said, trying to focus on something she'd kept secret from everyone. There was really only one thing. "I saw a ghost once. For real. When I stayed at my aunt's house."

In the darkness, Aveline couldn't see Hazel's reaction and waited for her to reply. She half expected her to laugh.

"What did the ghost want?" Hazel said eventually. "They all want something."

Aveline had thought about this a lot. "She didn't want to be alone."

There was another lengthy pause, before Hazel said, in a soft whisper, "I can understand that."

"So what about you?" Aveline asked. "What's your secret?"

Aveline waited for Hazel to answer. Time seemed to stretch on, until Aveline wondered if Hazel was actually going to answer at all. When she eventually did, she spoke in a low, halting voice, as if the words were stuck in her throat and she had to force them out into the open.

"I don't have a single friend in the whole world."

Aveline didn't know what to say. She understood what it felt like to be lonely. She'd had many occasions, sitting alone in her bedroom, when she'd wished she had a brother or sister to talk to. But at least she always had her mum, and she could pick up the phone and speak to her dad whenever she wanted. Harold was also there for her, plus she had a few mates at school. The way Hazel spoke, her words echoing slightly in this huge, empty house, made Aveline want to reach out and hug her.

"I'm your friend," she said.

"But you're going to leave soon, aren't you?" Hazel replied quietly.

"Maybe it's time you asked your parents for a phone then?" Aveline said, trying to lighten the mood. The conversation had turned as dark as the night outside. "Then we can talk whenever you like."

"It's not as easy as that."

As Aveline lay there, waiting to see if Hazel would explain what she meant, she heard Hazel's breathing slow and soften. That appeared to be her last word on the subject. But, as always, it left Aveline with more questions than answers.

Despite the size of the bed, the crispness of the sheets and the softness of the mattress, Aveline lay awake. So many thoughts jostled for attention. Had Hazel been exaggerating about not having any friends? Even in a small village like Norton Wick, surely there were people her own age? What about school friends? And were Hazel's parents regularly in the habit of leaving her on her own overnight? For a lonely girl, that would be the worst possible thing to do. It made Aveline feel scared. For herself and for Hazel, the girl who appeared to have everything. No wonder she'd been so keen to have company. While Aveline's mum had left her in their house alone before for an hour or two, Aveline knew she'd never, *ever* be left alone overnight.

Any suspicions about Hazel's unusual behaviour that may have lingered in Aveline's mind now felt unfounded. The only mystery here was how a girl who seemed to have so much could actually have so little.

At some point the questions must have stopped, because when Aveline next stirred, her sixth sense told her that it

must be some time in the middle of the night. A cold breeze fluttered against her eyelids. Hugging the sheets closer, she squeezed her eyes shut.

Before immediately opening them.

This wasn't a draught from an open window.

The window had gone.

The wind blew into the room unobstructed, lifting up her hair like ghostly fingers. By the light of the moon, she could see out towards the treeline and the fields beyond. Stars glittered coldly up above.

Alarmed, Aveline pushed herself up on one elbow. The plush cream carpet she'd walked in on had gone, too, revealing floorboards that didn't appear safe. They were nothing like the pristine hardwood floors in the rest of the house, which were so polished you could almost see your face in them. These were so rotten she wondered how the bed hadn't fallen through to the ground floor.

Then she noticed the smell.

A blend of ash, rot and damp; the house smelled like a bonfire after a rainy night. Pulling back the sheet, Aveline swung her feet out of bed before snatching back her hand in disgust. The sheets were like sails that had been pulled from an old fishing boat: coarse, damp and mottled with unpleasant stains.

Turning she saw Hazel, bundled beneath the covers. About to wake her, she noticed Hazel's eyes were open, two tiny pinpricks of light watching silently in the darkness.

"What are you doing?" Hazel said softly.

"What's going on?" Aveline said, turning to gesture to the crumbling, dirty space around them.

Only…Aveline realized that she wasn't looking at rickety wooden floorboards any more, but an expensive woollen carpet. Stretching out her feet, she tentatively allowed her toes to sink into its softness, banishing the sensation of cold and damp. Blinking, she gazed around in wonderment. The walls were as solid as a rock, the moonlight now shining through a window that had stylish curtains, open a fraction. The house appeared exactly as it had a few hours ago. She looked at it with wide eyes, as if seeing it for the very first time.

"Are you alright?" Hazel asked, pulling herself out from underneath the sheets.

Astonished, Aveline stared around the bedroom.

Ruffled Egyptian cotton sheets lay bunched where she'd climbed out of the huge bed.

"I don't know what happened," she said groggily. "I woke up and we were sleeping in the open, the bed was filthy, all the carpets had gone, and there were just rotten floorboards."

"I think you might be needing those," Hazel said, pointing to Aveline's glasses on the bedside table.

"I can still see okay without them," Aveline said, a little testily. "I swear, everything had gone... I don't understand."

"Nightmare, obviously. Too much ice cream, too late at night. That stuff does weird things, you know."

"I suppose it must have been," Aveline conceded. "It felt so real though."

"Waking nightmare," Hazel said. "I read about them once. People go walking about their houses, go outside, even speak to their family, but they're still dreaming."

"It's never happened to me before."

"You've probably never eaten a whole tub of rhubarb ice cream before bed either."

Aveline couldn't help but laugh, mostly from relief. The place she thought she'd been in hadn't felt nice at all. "Yeah, maybe I should cut back a little next time. Why were you awake anyway?"

"Someone pulled all the nice, warm sheets over to their side of the bed. Got a little chilly."

"Sorry."

"S'okay."

The girls said goodnight again. As she drew the sheets back over herself, Aveline inspected them closely, but couldn't find so much as a stray hair, let alone any stains. Relieved, she burrowed under them, but the memory of waking up in the cold, crumbling space refused to leave her mind for a long, sleepless time.

"She wished to measure the height of
a person and make a wax candle of that
height. And as the candle is consumed,
so will the person be consumed."

Church Court Archive, London, 1490.

Chapter 10
A Word of Warning

In the morning, Hazel woke Aveline with a gentle tap on the shoulder.

"Want some breakfast?" Hazel said, her eyes bright and hair shiny, as if she'd had the best, deepest sleep ever.

"Um…yeah," Aveline mumbled, her eyes crusty, her hair tousled, the disturbing nightmare having taken its toll.

"Pancakes, croissants, omelettes, bacon sandwiches, waffles, French toast, full English – what do you fancy?"

It all sounded so good. But then Aveline remembered that Harold would be waiting for her at the cottage.

"Actually, on second thoughts, I'd better be getting back," she said reluctantly, her stomach rumbling in dismay.

"You couldn't show me the way, could you? I sort of lost my bearings in the dark."

"Of course, I'll come with you," Hazel said.

"Don't you have to wait for your parents to come home?"

"No, it's fine, they said they'd be back later this morning sometime, not sure when exactly. I'll head back in a while. Wait here, I'll go and get dressed."

Aveline thought Hazel's parents must be the easiest-going people in the world, though something about the way Hazel was so vague about their whereabouts raised doubts, particularly remembering the sad way she'd spoken the previous night. It sounded like she'd made up it up on the spot. Aveline wasn't sure why Hazel would lie about her parents and what they were doing, but it made her ever so slightly uneasy.

A horrible thought came to mind: maybe Hazel's parents were neglecting her? That was the big mystery! It had to be. It would certainly explain some of her behaviour, such as why she appeared so keen to have company and was always free to do as she liked. Aveline wondered whether she should mention her concerns to her mum, but she didn't want to betray Hazel's confidence or get her into trouble if she'd got things wrong.

At the back of her mind, a plan took shape: she would

have to come here again when Hazel wasn't expecting her. With those big windows it would be easy to watch from the trees. Spying on someone wasn't nice, she knew that, but this was different. She would simply be looking out for her new friend. Hazel obviously felt unwilling to speak about her situation and this could be Aveline's only way of helping. All she needed to do was check that Hazel wasn't being left alone. She could bring Harold with her, too. He would love a top-secret mission. And if they saw that Hazel was being neglected then she would tell her mum immediately.

A few minutes later Hazel reappeared, looking as if she'd been dressed by a team of fashion stylists. As they left the house, Aveline glanced back, trying to see an approach road, but even in the daylight she couldn't see anything. The sky was a pale blue, the eastern horizon tinged pink where the sun was making its entrance. It felt chilly but refreshing.

"You know, Harold could be your friend, too, if you wanted," Aveline said. "He's really nice once you get to know him."

Hazel frowned, her kaleidoscope eyes narrowing. "You're the only friend I want, but thanks for the offer."

Her words sounded as if they were coated in ice.

"Um…okay."

Once again, Aveline had that unsettling feeling: that being friends with Hazel might bring with it a whole world of challenges.

As they crested a hill, Aveline caught sight of the church tower. Now she had her bearings. She could find her own way home from here, but didn't want Hazel to think she was pushing her away.

"You can come and have some breakfast at ours if you want."

"Okay, though I can only eat certain things or I get terribly ill."

"Really?"

"Yes. I'm limited to doughnuts, pancakes with syrup or chocolate croissants. It makes life very difficult."

Aveline laughed. It seemed Hazel's dark mood had passed and that made her happy. Her friend's temperament resembled the weather – cold one minute, warm the next. Slipping her arm into the crook of Hazel's elbow, she yanked her into a jog.

"Okay, only you might have to settle for cornflakes. Croissants are a bit too fancy for us."

"Fine, as long as I can put chocolate spread on them," Hazel said with a grin.

As they passed the lychgate that led into St Michael's church, they saw Alice tramping through the graveyard in her big boots.

"Oh no, quick, run!" Hazel hissed, giving Aveline's arm an almighty yank.

Giggling, Aveline began to run alongside Hazel. Together they fled down the lane, towards The Witch Stones and the cottage, the fresh morning breeze fanning their glowing cheeks. It felt fun to be staging a grand escape from the strange vicar at the church, but even so, Aveline glanced back, unable to suppress a twinge of guilt.

Alice stood in the lychgate, watching them sprint along the lane. Her mouth hung open, and her normally rosy face had turned as pale as the morning light. She looked equally alarmed and shocked. Aveline took all this in for a brief instant, before she turned back so she could see where she was going.

"I-I think she saw us," Aveline gasped.

"Good! I don't care, the old hag's just jealous!" Hazel cried.

Flushed from their exertions, they arrived back at the cottage and barged in through the door.

"Morning, Mum!" Aveline yelled.

Harold sat alone at the kitchen table, cereal spoon in

one hand, book in another, his fringe dangling over his eyes like a giant eyelash. Glancing up, he broke into a wide grin.

"My name's actually Harold, but you can call me Mum if you like. They've all popped out for a walk around the village."

Aveline laughed, though she couldn't help but notice that Hazel didn't.

"I've changed my mind about breakfast," Hazel said. "I'm going to go eat back home. I'll see you later."

"You sure?"

"Yeah. See you, Harold."

"Bye," Harold said, hand raised. He waited a moment for Hazel to leave before looking up at Aveline with a pained expression. "I don't think she likes me, Aveline, and I wish I knew why."

"She's just shy, I think," Aveline said, trying to find a reason why Hazel seemed to make so little effort to get on with him.

"Shy?" Harold said, with a snort. "You could have fooled me. She's the most confident person I've ever met!"

"I think that's just an act. You know how it is with some people. They put on a show because deep down inside, they're actually really nervous."

"Mmm…I don't think she knows what the word means," Harold muttered, spooning in a huge mouthful of cereal. Aveline couldn't help but notice that he appeared to have spilled as much on the kitchen table as he'd got in his mouth. "What was it like then, did you have a good night?"

"It was strange, if I'm honest. Very strange. And that's part of the reason why I think she's putting on an act. Promise you won't tell my mum, but her parents weren't there. It was just the two of us. I think she might be being neglected."

Harold stopped mid-chew. A trickle of milk ran down one side of his mouth and he wiped it away with his sleeve. "Seriously?"

Aveline related all that had happened the previous evening – from their hunt for the witches' grave and the strange encounter in the graveyard with Alice, to her unsettling experience in the middle of the night. She left out the confession that Hazel had made about not having any friends. That felt secret. Something that shouldn't be shared.

"So we have to go back there. Later today. We have to check that she's not being left alone all the time."

"Why not just tell your mum when she gets back?"

Harold asked, getting up to dump his bowl in the sink.

"Because it might be nothing, that's why. Maybe Hazel's parents thought she'd be fine on her own for one night because I would be there to keep her company. People have different rules and, I don't know, maybe they're just more relaxed about things like that in the country?"

"Maybe. Okay, we can go down later. I'll bring my binoculars, they're perfect for spying…I mean, checking on people."

Aveline heard him thump upstairs like a baby elephant, hoping the withered wooden stairs wouldn't give way underneath him. She unpacked her overnight bag, silently cursing as she realized she'd left her toothbrush at Hazel's. Grabbing herself some juice from the fridge, she heard her mum talking outside and went to open the door. Her mum, along with Aunt Lilian and Mr Lieberman, were in conversation with someone at the garden gate.

As Aveline drew nearer, she saw that they were talking to Alice. She'd removed her hat, which she used to fan her plump cheeks, red in the heat of the morning.

"…and we have some fine stained-glass windows depicting scenes from both the Old and New Testament – you'll have to come down and have a look."

"We most certainly will," Mr Lieberman said, who'd also removed his trilby in the warm weather. "We may even take a walk down this afternoon if that's amenable?"

"Oh, you know churches," Alice replied, her eyes straying towards Aveline. "We're open all hours. I see Aveline has come to join us. I don't think she's seen *inside* the church yet either."

Aveline blushed at Alice's subtle reference to their previous meeting. She suddenly felt guilty again about running away from her earlier. As if she'd done something cruel.

"Ah, the wanderer returns," Aunt Lilian said.

"Morning, love," Aveline's mum said. "How was your night with Hazel?"

"Oh, fine, thanks," Aveline said, the lie coming effortlessly.

"Well, come in and have some breakfast if you haven't already. Alice, would you care to join us for a cup of tea?"

"Oh, I'm afraid I must attend to church business. Maybe another time if the offer still stands?"

"Of course."

As the three adults made their way into the cottage, Alice touched Aveline's sleeve. "Could I have a quick word, Aveline?"

Reluctantly, Aveline nodded. Joining Alice under the welcome shade of the apple tree, she waited to hear what she had to say. Undoubtedly it wasn't going to be something good. She bowed her head, adopting the body language of someone who's about to be told off.

"Forgive me, Aveline, I know you must have things to do. But it's something your mum just said. She said you'd stayed with a girl called Hazel last night. That's the girl I saw you with earlier, isn't it?"

Aveline wished a hole in the ground would open up underneath her. "I'm sorry we ran away without saying hello," she cut in. "We were late and had to rush."

"I don't care about that, Aveline. Believe me when I say people regularly go out of their way to avoid my company." Mopping her brow with a handkerchief, Alice smiled, her red cheeks rising up to meet her eyes. "Do you remember what I said when we spoke yesterday?"

"Yes, of course. You said not to get into trouble and to trust my intuition."

"And what does your intuition tell you about Hazel, may I ask?"

"You know her then?" Aveline said, fiddling with her glasses.

"Yes, I happen to know Hazel very well," Alice continued. "But do you?"

Aveline wasn't sure what to say, but there was something about Alice's honest, open expression that invited the truth. "Well, yes, I think so – although I haven't known her for long, it's true. But I really like her. She's funny and smart. Only, I don't think she's very happy."

"That's very astute of you, Aveline. Hazel is, indeed, a wonderfully gifted but very troubled girl. That's why I would counsel you to keep your distance, otherwise you may find yourself caught up in matters you don't understand."

"But how am I supposed to help her if I don't see her?"

"I'm going to be here for her, Aveline, as I always have been, and you can rest assured that I do everything in my power to look after her. Of course, that presents its challenges. I'm afraid Hazel doesn't have a very high opinion of me."

No, she thinks you're a witch, Aveline thought.

"But let me reassure you that Hazel is very much cared for. The best way *you* can help is by giving her a wide berth. She's not like…other girls, you see." Alice paused, clenching her teeth as if unsure how to continue. "I know this must all sound very odd, Aveline, but you'll have to trust me on this one. Keep your distance, for your own sake. I know what I'm doing, even if appearances may suggest otherwise. Good day to you!"

Aveline watched Alice clump away, before walking slowly back up the garden path and into the cottage. So Hazel and Alice knew each other? That was odd. Hazel hadn't given Aveline that impression at all. But if Alice truly was a witch, and *she knew* that Hazel knew, then maybe she was trying to force them apart on purpose?

Despite everything Alice had said, Aveline couldn't just abandon Hazel. Last night she'd assured Hazel that she was her friend. And friends stuck together through thick and thin.

No, as far as Aveline was concerned, the plan was still on. She and Harold would go and find out what was really happening at Hazel's house. You didn't help people by avoiding them.

As she made her way back into the cottage, Harold met her at the bottom of the stairs.

"Got them," he said, holding up a small pair of binoculars. "I knew they'd come in handy. But you wouldn't believe what else I found while you were out last night. This was tucked away at the back of a cupboard. Pretty creepy if you ask me."

In his other hand, he held up an old, battered pamphlet, yellowed with age. On the cover was old-fashioned lettering, along with a rather unsettling picture of a woman riding a sow. The title said:

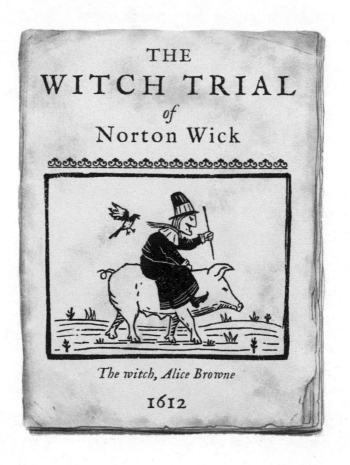

THE
WITCH TRIAL
of
Norton Wick

The witch, Alice Browne

1612

"This, believe it or not, is an actual account of the trial that happened here," Harold said breathlessly. "It's hard to make out what's going on because it's written in a really weird way, but I reckon we need to try and give it a read, like, as soon as possible."

Aveline took it from him for a closer look. A sickly feeling crept up from her stomach to the back of her throat. Because underneath the image of the woman on the sow there was a caption.

The witch, Alice Browne.

It was spelled Browne with an *e*.

"Who does not understand,
should either learn, or be silent."

*Dr John Dee, Astrologer to
Queen Elizabeth I, 1527–1608.*

Chapter 11
Shadows of the Past

The evening was misty and humid, like walking through the steam from a kettle. Harold and Aveline had left the adults inside watching TV. They'd said they wouldn't be too long or too late, and everybody had been happy with that. Now, as they approached the church, the sinking sun gave it an orange blush, as if it were made from gingerbread and not cold, grey stone.

Aveline wondered if Alice was inside. And what she was doing.

"Are you alright?" Harold said. "You look a bit queasy."

"N-no, I'm fine," Aveline said. "Just a bit tired, that's all. Thanks for coming with me tonight – though I'm not entirely sure I'll be able to find Hazel's house again."

"Of course you will," Harold reassured her. "How many huge houses made of glass can there be in little old Norton Wick?"

Aveline's gaze turned back towards the church. She could see a faint glow from the vestry window. The pamphlet that Harold had showed her about the witch trial bothered her a great deal. Not just the fact that they'd actually put somebody on trial here, though that felt awful enough. But the name of the witch on the cover seemed an odd coincidence to say the least – a combination of the names of the only two people she'd come to know since arriving here.

Aveline couldn't ever remember Alice revealing her surname, and just because Hazel's was spelled the same way as the witch's – Browne with an e – well, that didn't mean anything other than it just happened to be a common local name. Yet only last night, Hazel had taken her to what she claimed was the site of the witches' grave. Once again, Aveline had that niggling sensation that she was closing in on something that didn't want to be revealed. It felt like the moment just before you walked through the door into a new school, when the sense of fearful excitement became almost overwhelming.

Hurrying on, with Harold following close behind,

Aveline eventually found a stile that led into a field. She remembered climbing over it, and there being a narrow path. Sure enough, there it was, trailing through the wheat stalks. After a longish walk, they crested the brow of a hill and paused to get their bearings. Down below in the valley, Aveline could see a thick copse of trees that looked familiar. Hazel's house had been surrounded by trees and, with no other woodland visible in any direction, it seemed the likeliest option.

"It must be down there. Behind those trees."

"Wait a minute," Harold said, raising his binoculars to his face. For a few moments he scanned them left and right. "Apart from a suspicious-looking cow, the coast appears to be clear," he said. Raising his arm, he gestured in a forward motion. "Let's move out."

"Harold," Aveline sighed. "We're just checking on Hazel, not sneaking behind enemy lines."

"We still have to be careful. It's not going to look very good if Hazel catches us spying on her, is it? I wouldn't want to get on the wrong side of her."

Nor me, Aveline thought. Something about Hazel's strong personality suggested that, as well as being a great friend, she could probably make a bitter enemy, too.

They hiked down towards the trees, the grassy tussocks

making their footsteps springy and light, like they were bouncing on a trampoline. Reaching the treeline, they made their way into the shadows. This was the place. Aveline was sure of it. Shielded from the hazy evening sun, the cool woody space made Aveline shiver, as if she'd stepped outside the everyday world into a darker place.

Suddenly they emerged back into the light of a clearing, and Aveline blinked, realizing she *must* have lost her way.

In front of them stood the ruins of an old farmhouse.

The roof had collapsed, revealing an interior filled with rubble and cracked tiles. Blackened beams resembled the ribs of a giant skeleton. Aveline was confused. She'd been positive that this was where she'd stayed the night, only it must have been a hundred years since this cottage had been in a fit state for someone to sleep in, maybe more.

"Oh," was all she could say.

"Not exactly a millionaire's house, is it?" Harold said, though she noticed that he didn't say it with his usual grin. He could sense that something wasn't quite right, too.

They walked closer. The building's blackened interior suggested that perhaps fire, and not age, had been

responsible for its demise. Aveline thought she could still detect a very faint smell of ash. The door was long gone, so Aveline stepped straight through the open doorway into what had once been the interior. Nature had reclaimed most of it, the fireplace where people might have gathered now only drew the company of nettles and dock leaves. For a while they explored, kicking stones and branches to one side just in case they were concealing anything of interest, but the cottage seemed long abandoned.

Then Aveline saw a flash of colour, its neon pink a striking contrast to the dull, earthy shades of wood, stone and weed. Aveline knew immediately what it was. Even so, she bent down for a closer look, wanting to make doubly sure.

Her toothbrush.

She'd last seen it yesterday evening at Hazel's. She could clearly remember where she'd left it – on the side of the expensive marble sink in the en-suite bathroom. So either it had been brought here by someone, maybe Hazel, and dropped into the old ruin...which seemed a strange thing to do... Or, stranger still...this was actually the place she'd stayed in. Aveline recalled her frightening experience in the middle of the night, when she'd woken to find herself inside a derelict house. Hazel had said it must have been a vivid nightmare, but the reality appeared to be far more terrifying than any dream.

"It's called a *glamour*."

Hazel's voice cut through the stillness. Turning, Aveline saw her standing some way off, underneath the trees. In the half-light, she seemed to shimmer unnaturally, like the glow of a lamp on a winter night.

"What's a glamour?" Aveline asked Hazel nervously, suddenly aware that she and Harold were alone with Hazel and nobody knew where they'd gone. Why that should bother her, she didn't exactly know.

But it did.

"It's a spell, of sorts," Hazel said, stepping out of the trees. "It makes things appear more attractive than they are, and this house certainly needs all the help it can get, don't you think?"

"Harold, maybe we should head back," Aveline whispered, watching Hazel move towards them. "Harold?"

Turning, she saw him standing stock-still in the ruins. His head was bowed, his fringe drooping down over his face like the branches of a weeping willow. His arms hung limply and, unless she was mistaken, Aveline thought she could hear him gently snoring.

"Harold?" Aveline said again, louder this time.

"He's fine," Hazel said. She stood much closer now, almost at Aveline's shoulder. "I just thought it'd be better if we could talk alone for a while."

"What have you done to him?"

"I've just put him to sleep for a few minutes. No need to worry. I can wake him any time you like, but let's talk for a while first, please."

Running over to where Harold stood, Aveline grabbed him by the shoulders and gave him a shake. She stared into his heavy-lidded eyes – they were glazed and unfocused.

"Promise me he's okay?"

"It's just like he's having an afternoon nap."

Aveline studied Harold, biting her lower lip, not quite ready to take Hazel's word for it. So this was what real magic looked like. No tricks, no sleight of hand, but some kind of immensely powerful charm that had left Harold almost zombie-like. Aveline shivered, feeling the hairs on her arm tingle. Right now, she needed to take things one very careful step at a time, for Harold's sake as much as her own.

Hazel sat down and crossed her legs. Then she plucked a daisy from the grass and began pulling off its petals one by one. Aveline heard her whispering to herself.

"She loves me...she loves me not..."

"Okay, let's talk," Aveline said. "This *is* your house then?"

"Yes, it used to be. A long time ago. After they took us away, nobody dared live here and eventually somebody burned it down."

Aveline frowned. She had no idea who *they* were. Truth be told, she had no idea who Hazel was any more. Certainly not the girl she thought she knew. Her magic spells at the stones had been one thing. Conjuring up a gigantic illusion and putting people to sleep was in a different league. She remembered what Alice had said.

Hazel's not like other girls.

"You don't..." Hesitating, Aveline struggled to find the right words. "You don't have any parents, do you?"

Throwing the daisy stalk away, Hazel hugged her knees, which made her look scared and vulnerable. Immediately, all Aveline's nervousness melted away and she walked over, kneeled down and took Hazel by the hand.

"Who are you really, Hazel?"

The mismatched eyes locked onto Aveline's and for a moment she saw them widen in fear, before hardening into a cool, appraising gaze.

"You knew something wasn't quite right, didn't you, Aveline? See, I knew you were smart when I first met you. That's why I'm glad we're friends. We should be friends for ever."

Aveline snuck another glance at Harold, who still hadn't moved. It shocked her, seeing him staring at the ground like a zombie. She had to help him, but she wasn't sure how. All she did know was not to antagonize Hazel, who might have even worse tricks up her sleeve. Aveline had to soothe her, settle her down, and persuade her to return Harold to normal.

"Why don't you tell me who you really are?" Aveline repeated, as calmly as she could. "If we're going to continue being friends then I need to know."

"If I tell you," Hazel said, "will you promise not to hate me? People tend to get the wrong idea."

"Of course I won't hate you," Aveline said. "I could never hate you."

"Come over here then and I'll show you."

Hazel got up and led Aveline around the side of the ruined cottage, towards a small stone trough. The green water inside smelled dank and earthy. Hazel perched herself on the edge and motioned for Aveline to come and sit beside her, which she did, checking that she could still see Harold and that he was okay. Every few seconds he would twitch, as if he was having a bad dream, but he seemed as well as any enchanted person could be.

"A mirror would be better," Hazel explained, as if this was all very run-of-the-mill. "But I can use any surface you can see your reflection in. This'll have to do. All you have to do is look down into the water and not get scared."

Trailing a finger back and forth across the water's surface, Hazel murmured under her breath, her voice slow and dreamy.

"Shadows of the past, let me see you."

At first nothing happened, and Aveline suppressed a nervous giggle. Then the air seemed to thicken, as if it had turned to smoke, and images began to appear in the water like it had just been tuned into a TV channel. Gasping, Aveline leaned in closer.

The first thing Aveline saw were two figures kneeling in a gloomy wood, pulling plants and roots from the soil. One was a girl about her age, the other a woman. Both had long dark hair.

The water rippled and the image changed. The same two now sat in front of a hearth. The woman added herbs to a simmering metal pot suspended above a fire. The girl sat to one side, plucking leaves from a small twig. As she watched, the girl laid the twig to one side and stood up. The firelight illuminated her features. Flowing black hair and bronzed skin. A gracefulness in the simplest of movements.

Hazel.

Even as Aveline realized who this was, the girl in the image glanced in Aveline's direction, almost as if she knew somebody was watching her. Her eyes flashed as they caught the firelight, one green and one blue.

Hazel trailed a finger across the surface of the water again and now Aveline could see men on horseback, galloping through the field of the standing stones. They wore wide-brimmed hats and their stern, whiskered faces spoke of a grim business to come. Somehow Aveline understood that these men were looking for the two women. A feeling of utter terror gripped her, unlike any she had ever experienced before.

Then, in the rippling surface of the trough, she saw Hazel and the older woman crying and reaching out to one another as they were marched by burly men through the stone circle. A large group of villagers stood on the fallen stones, shaking their fists and shouting insults as the women were led towards the tall oak tree in the far part of the field. Hanging from one of its branches...thick ropes with nooses at the end swayed in the breeze.

Panic swelled in Aveline's throat and she felt sick, fear curdling her insides. She dropped to her knees, unable to watch any longer. Her breaths battled to escape her body, every muscle twitched and tensed, as if she herself was struggling to break free. Somehow, she was there, with the women, feeling and sharing their fear. As the world around her darkened, her vision blurred and she fell into the grass, her feet jerking in fitful movements, as though she was dancing.

"And after this he appeared to her in other shapes: as sometimes of a brown coloured dog, sometimes as a white cat, and at other times like a hare."

Lancaster Witch Trial, 1634.

Chapter 12
An Offer You Can't Refuse

Aveline had never known relief like it. Opening her eyes, it felt like she was seeing the world for the first time and she gulped down the sweet, summer night air like water. The treetops swayed in the breeze, the birds sang melodiously and a hand gently touched her forehead. It felt like the cool flannel her mum placed on her skin when she had a fever. As she struggled up on her elbows, she saw Hazel staring back at her. Immediately, she pushed her away.

"What did you do to me?"

"Nothing. I just showed you what happened to us, many years ago. You felt it, too. Turns out you're sensitive to things, Aveline, like me. Do you ever get feelings about people and places that you just can't explain, as if a voice in your head is whispering secrets to you?"

Aveline nodded. She had. She did. But right now, her thoughts turned to her friend.

"Where's Harold?" Even as she clambered to her feet, she could see him still gently swaying in the ruins, like a scarecrow stuck on a pole in a summer breeze. Tears blurred her vision, but she didn't know why she was so upset. It felt as if someone very precious had been taken away from her.

"I want to go now," Aveline said. "Can you make Harold normal again, please, so that we can leave?"

"I thought you promised not to hate me," Hazel said softly.

"I don't hate you," Aveline gasped. "I'm scared of what you've done to Harold."

"There's no need to be," Hazel said. "I thought you trusted me?"

Blinking the tears away, Aveline pulled off her glasses and gave them a wipe, trying to clear her thoughts. "I don't know what to think any more," she said. "But I'm sorry something horrible happened to you."

Hazel took Aveline by the arms. Her distinctive eyes glistened as tears brimmed in them. "It's okay, don't be upset. I've had a few hundred years to get over it."

A loud giggle broke through Aveline's tears. She couldn't believe she was laughing. By rights she should have been screaming. Curious, she squeezed Hazel's arms. They were as real and warm as her own.

"But if something bad happened to you hundreds of years ago," Aveline said, carefully avoiding the word *died*, "what are you doing here, today, standing in front of me?"

"We're trapped here," Hazel hissed, a spark of anger flashing across her face. "It wasn't enough that they executed us, just for having a little knowledge of the old ways. Our *punishment* continued after we were dead, too, so after they dragged our bodies from the stone circle, they buried us in the bad soil, at the north of the church. Rest is for others, but not for us."

"So that was *your* grave you showed me?"

"Yes. Not much to look at, is it?"

Aveline thought back to what she now knew was a witch bottle. She remembered Hazel's yelp of pain when she'd first come to the cottage and her eagerness to make Aveline get rid of it; the way she'd leaped gleefully into the garden the minute it'd been smashed.

"So…you are a witch?"

"Some might call us that – those who are afraid of things they don't understand."

"Who's the other woman, Hazel? The one I saw in the water? You keep referring to *us* all the time." Even as she asked the question, the answer presented itself in Aveline's mind. "It's Alice, isn't it?" she said. "You're Hazel Browne and she's Alice Browne...she's your mother!"

"Almost right, Aveline, but not quite. She's my sister."

"Sisters?" Aveline said, her eyes wide behind her glasses. "But Alice looks so different now? And why do you always say horrible things about her if she's your family?"

"Yes, strange, isn't it? I mean, why would you cut all your hair off and start wearing a bowler hat?" Hazel snorted, her top lip curling in disdain. "Especially when she could take on any appearance she liked, if she really wanted. You see, I'm afraid our sisterly love quickly turned sour after what happened. We want different things. And now she chooses to spend all her time creeping around a church, polishing candlesticks and singing dreary hymns. More fool her. Anyway, now you know it all. So tell me, why did you come looking for me at the house?"

"We wanted to make sure you were alright. I thought you were being left on your own, neglected. Silly, I suppose."

Hazel touched her again on the arm. "No, it's kind – but you needn't have worried. Despite Alice sticking her nose in occasionally, I've been on my own for a long time. Almost longer than I care to remember. Still, *you're* here now, aren't you?"

"Yes," Aveline said, her voice a little · shaky. She couldn't think about this any more. She just wanted to get herself and Harold back to the cottage and normality, where mums made hot drinks and aunts watched TV and witches only existed in books. She needed time and space to take all of this in. "I don't suppose you could wake Harold up now, could you? We really should be getting back."

Shaking her long black hair, Hazel walked slowly over to where Harold still snoozed. With one hand she flicked at his fringe. Something about the way Hazel treated Harold as a plaything made Aveline nervous.

"You know, Aveline, I think I prefer him like this. I could use him to hang my coats on."

"Please, Hazel," Aveline insisted.

"I'll do it," Hazel said. "Only..." Pausing, she wound a

finger through Harold's hair, which was something Harold would often do himself. "I want you to do something for me in return."

"What do you want me to do?"

"Stay with me."

"I can't right now, we need to get home," Aveline stammered. "My mum will be getting worried."

"I don't mean right now. I mean stay with me, here, in Norton Wick. I'm lonely, Aveline. You don't know what it's like. Imagine being all alone for hundreds of years, nobody to talk to, nowhere to go. I can never leave this village and I don't want to be here on my own any more."

"But you've got your sister Alice – why do you need me?" Aveline cried, shaking her head as if to shut out these words that made no sense. "I can't just wander off and spend my days running around with you."

"Alice might as well be dead to me. But you wouldn't believe the sort of life *we* could have together, Aveline. We can do *anything* we want. Live in total luxury, eat and drink what we like, wear beautiful clothes, ride horses and eat rhubarb ice cream for breakfast, lunch and dinner – whatever we like, and I mean that. I can make you the happiest girl alive."

"But you're not really…alive, are you?"

Hazel paused.

"I am and I'm not. But it isn't a problem, it's an advantage. And I can make you the same as me."

"What?"

"You give something up and you get something in return. Just like at the stones. And that's what we'll do. If you give up your normal, boring life, you can live for ever, here, with me."

"I don't want to give up my life! I want to live and grow up. I don't want to be twelve for ever." Aveline couldn't believe what she was hearing. Hazel made it all sound so casual.

"You don't have to be. We can be any age we like. You can still see your mum and your aunt and the old bookseller. You can even see Harold if you really have to. We'll make the rules up as we go along."

"Honestly, Hazel, I just want to be normal, like everybody else. Now, please will you wake Harold up?"

"Suit yourself." Hazel gave a flick of her hand, as if she was swatting away a fly. Then, turning to Aveline, she seemed to grow larger and taller, her raven hair flowing upwards and outwards as if lifted by a strong breeze. "You know, I can make your life wonderful, Aveline. But maybe I need to change your mind another way."

"What do you mean?" Aveline asked, sensing the unmistakeable threat in Hazel's words.

"Oh, you know, make you see what life's like when you can't rely on the people you trust the most. Anyway, I'll see you soon. Please don't mention our little conversation to anyone. And thanks for popping over to the house. Sorry I didn't have time to clean up."

Laughing, Hazel walked away into the trees, leaving Aveline shivering despite the late evening warmth. Not long ago, the thought of being best friends for ever with Hazel would have delighted her. Now it made her skin ripple with fear.

"Well, there's nothing much going on here. I suppose we should be getting home." Harold stood in the ruins, looking as wide awake as she'd ever seen him. Shrugging his shoulders, he walked towards her. "Come on, let's go before it gets dark. This place gives me the creeps."

"Magpies have often been associated with ill fortune."

Guide to Birds of the British Isles, *1964*.

Chapter 13
Tale of Two Sisters

Harold seemed none the worse for his ordeal. He chatted all the way back, mainly offering his theories on why they had got lost and which direction they could try tomorrow in an effort to find Hazel's house. Aveline desperately wanted to tell him what had really happened, but Hazel had forbidden her from telling anyone and she didn't take that order lightly. Not now she knew the truth. Besides, what could she say? That Hazel was actually a witch who had been killed hundreds of years ago but somehow survived? That her sister was the local vicar? It sounded so far-fetched it almost made Aveline want to laugh.

Yet as they wandered back towards the church and the

village, Aveline felt she needed to speak to somebody. And really, there was only one person who would understand.

"You go on ahead, Harold, I'm just popping into the church. I think I left something there when me and Hazel came the other night. Tell Mum to put some hot chocolate on."

"Okay," Harold replied. "If you're not back in five minutes, I'll assume you've been stuck in a cauldron and boiled up with some carrots."

Aveline watched him go. Despite herself, she kept thinking about Hazel's offer. Even though a tiny part of her was curious, tempted even, she didn't believe what Hazel had told her about living for ever. It just wasn't possible. Harold would grow old but she wouldn't. How would that work?

Above the gravestones, a rising harvest moon glowed an unearthly red. A gasp caught in Aveline's chest. In some way it felt like a warning, telling her that life had ceased to be normal and predictable. Moons were not white any more. Witches were not fairy tales.

Reaching the lychgate, Aveline ran down the side of the church, towards the north end. The vestry lights burned brightly. It appeared Alice might be inside.

Pausing, Aveline took a deep breath. If Hazel was to be believed, she was about to knock on the door of a centuries-old witch. What would Alice say when she realized Aveline knew her secret? Sighing, she knocked on the side door and waited. She had to trust her instincts on this one: Alice wasn't out to get her, or anyone else.

A few seconds later, Aveline heard a lock slide back and Alice peered out.

"Aveline, hello there. Somehow I thought it'd be you. What's happened? I can tell by your rather anxious demeanour that something's amiss."

"I just spoke to Hazel. I know what happened to her and that you're...her sister."

Alice's face crumpled, as if she'd just walked out into a biting wind.

"Oh, I see. The cat's out of the bag, is it? Come on in then. I expect you'll be wanting an explanation."

Glancing nervously behind her just to check that Hazel wasn't watching, Aveline entered, noticing with a little alarm that Alice closed and locked the heavy wooden door. Inside, the vestry smelled of candle wax and lilies. On a large wooden desk lay a mishmash of old books, notebooks and parchments with strange writing and symbols scrawled on them. A pencil drawing on the wall depicted The Witch Stones, with figures in white robes standing inside them. Not the kind of picture Aveline expected to see in a church. Other than the desk, the picture, a couple of chairs and a cupboard, the vestry room was bare, but not unwelcoming.

"Can I get you a drink? I promise it won't turn you into a toad."

Aveline couldn't help but return Alice's smile. "No, I'm okay, thanks."

"Well, at least have a seat. Get some colour back into your cheeks."

Settling herself into the chair opposite, Alice took a sip from a small glass of amber liquid. Swallowing, she grimaced. "So, tell me everything."

Aveline told her what had happened – about how she and Harold had gone to look for the house and about what Hazel had told – and showed – her.

"And now she wants me to stay with her for ever. To be a witch, too, I suppose. Like both of you. That's true, isn't it – you are a witch?"

Alice raised her eyebrows. "Yes, it's true, though witches aren't always what you might think. Labels are complicated matters." Alice sighed. "To some, a witch is an evil thing. To others, they're nothing more than a person who's willing to explore unconventional forms of knowledge."

"What sort of witch are you?" Aveline said, almost gasping out her question.

"Oh, certainly not a witch who wishes to harm anyone. However, I have encountered others in our tradition who had altogether darker intentions. Currently, I'd say Hazel falls somewhere in the middle. That's why I've settled here, in the church, so I can keep an eye on the village and its inhabitants and make sure Hazel doesn't follow through on some of the threats she's made."

"She wants to hurt people?"

"She's full of anger, Aveline, about what the ancestors of this village did to us, and it's never left her. But in truth, her real anger is directed at me. I don't want revenge, you see. Neither do I want to manipulate others. And Hazel resents that. She wanted us to become a kind of terrible sisterhood, to grow in power and influence until everybody cowered before us. Only, I didn't. It's as simple as that. And although I've been trying to persuade her over to my way of thinking, I'm unable to build any bridges. Her rage is too fierce, like a fiery ball inside her that burns oh-so brightly. So we're what you might call *estranged*. Fortunately, I've managed to foil some of her more sinister plans over the centuries, but she still likes to wreak a little havoc across the village from time to time."

"This is all so…bizarre," Aveline said, struggling to find words that made sense of her jumbled thoughts. Instinctively, she stepped nearer the door.

"Yes, super weird, isn't it?" Alice said with a grimace, seeming to sense Aveline's nervousness. "But trust me, Aveline, you – or anyone else, for that matter – are in no danger from me. You can forgive and forget a lot when you've lived for as long as we have. The people who did this were full of hate and ignorance and thankfully they're dead and gone – a fact Hazel seems unable, or unwilling, to accept."

"That's another thing I don't understand: how are you both here if you're both…you know…dead?"

"We were killed at one of the most powerful magical sites in this country. Oh yes, Aveline, don't believe those fairy tales about dancing witches being turned to stone – Hazel and I are how The Witch Stones *really* got their name, though there's nobody around any more to admit to it. And unbeknownst to the bloodthirsty mob that dragged us away, taking our life at the stones and then burying us here, in the darkness, created a bond between us and the land hereabouts that even death can't break.

So now Hazel and I are stuck between this life and the next. The best way I can describe it is to imagine yourself as a shadow. You're there and you're real and you exist in this world. But at the same time, you're not as real as the people who cast those shadows. And the same rules that apply to people don't apply to shadows."

Aveline shuddered. "I never want to live like that."

Alice forced a grim smile and scratched her bristly salt-and-pepper hair. "That doesn't surprise me. I don't want to either and all my efforts are focused on finding a way that we can be at peace. You've seen me at work over in the stones. I think I'm getting closer, too. We're subject to very powerful magic and breaking free of that requires time, study and a great deal of patience. Hazel, on the other hand, seems to enjoy certain aspects of our odd existence and is no help whatsoever. I can say from personal experience that it's not a path on which *you'll* find any kind of happiness."

"Can she truly make me the same as you?"

"I'm not sure, Aveline. But I'd rather you didn't try and find out."

"What will she do if I don't agree to stay with her?"

Clambering to her feet with a soft groan, Alice helped herself to another drink. "One thing I've learned, Aveline, is that you always have a choice. All you have to do is tell her that you're not interested."

"I have! Only, she didn't seem to like my answer. What if she gets angry and tries to force me?" Aveline hadn't forgotten Hazel's thinly veiled threat.

"If that's the case, and part of me isn't surprised by her reaction, then I can help you. Despite her formidable talents, Hazel has her weak spots, just like anyone. For one, she's unable to come into your cottage. I helped the owners make a charm there, many moons ago. Hazel had taken a particular dislike to them."

Grimacing, Aveline squeezed the fingers of one hand in the palm of the other. "Um…I think I might have broken it." Sheepishly, she related how she'd found the bottle, and how Hazel had persuaded her to smash it.

"Oh, she's a crafty one," Alice said, in a manner that suggested a sisterly pride. "But no matter, we can make another."

"Now?" Aveline asked. The thought of having some protection sounded very appealing.

"Actually, when I said *we* can make one, I meant *you*," Alice replied. "It's for your protection so you need to gather it all together, and soon. But don't look so anxious, I can help you, just like I helped them."

Alice began riffling through the pile of papers and books on her desk, pausing occasionally to frown at something before throwing it back down. Eventually, she drew out a small, leather-bound book, blew the dust off the cover and handed it to Aveline.

"Here. Just think of it as a recipe."

"And it'll work?"

"Hopefully," Alice said, which wasn't quite the confident answer Aveline had wished for. Seeing Aveline's face drop, Alice added, "As long as you follow the instructions correctly. And don't forget the herbs I gave you, too, they're bound to come in handy."

"I don't want to hurt her," Aveline said, remembering the pain in Hazel's foot when she had tried to come into the cottage's garden.

"Sometimes extreme circumstances require extreme solutions. But don't worry, her pride will be hurt more than her body. Just take a few sensible magical precautions and all will be well, and you can leave Norton Wick with nothing more than memories of a happy holiday. I think you have a talent for our line of work, Aveline, which is probably why Hazel likes you so much. Meanwhile, I shall make sure to keep an extra sharp lookout on your behalf. Now, you best get yourself home."

Aveline said goodnight and set off. The moon had risen a little, losing its eerie red hue. The countryside had turned from scarlet to silver, thin shadows stretching over the fields while the stars flickered up above. Aveline took the path that led to the rear of the cottage. Almost at the back gate, she stopped in her tracks. She sensed Hazel's presence. She recognized the signs: a tingle of electricity in the air; the sensation of being watched or followed; an inexplicable nervousness in her tummy, as if her body was making up its mind whether to be sick or not. Sure enough, she heard Hazel's voice, a hiss on the breeze.

"I see you've been talking with Alice. What have you two been plotting?"

"Nothing, she was just trying to help me understand things," Aveline said, tucking the book behind her back. Turning, Aveline expected to see Hazel's wicked smirk and gleaming eyes. Only this time, she couldn't see anybody. "Hazel, where are you?"

"We can do this together soon."

"What?"

"Become invisible. Do what nobody

else can. Imagine that, Aveline, being able to go wherever you like, without anybody knowing you're there. We can even take on the form of animals and birds for short periods. Just wait until you feel what flying is like, it'll blow your mind!"

Aveline remembered the magpie that was often hanging around before Hazel made an appearance. Shiny feathers, a glint in the eye and always up to mischief. It made total sense.

"As long as we don't fly outside of Norton Wick though, right?"

"Don't be mean, Aveline, it doesn't suit you."

"Well, it's hard to hold a conversation with thin air."

A hand gripped Aveline's shoulder and gave it a painful squeeze.

"That solid enough for you?"

As Hazel appeared from behind a stone, Aveline caught her breath. Hazel oozed witchery, clad in a long, flowing black dress, with wide bell sleeves that cascaded down over her wrists. Caught in the breeze, her dress rustled and rippled like a cloud scudding over the moon, giving her a truly magical appearance.

"So, are you excited?"

Aveline pushed her spectacles back. "About what?"

"You know, about staying here with me."

"Hazel, you know I can't stay here for ever."

"Of course you can. You can do anything you like. It's your decision to make. Hasn't anybody ever told you that? But maybe I just need to convince you a little more."

Sighing, Hazel reached out to embrace Aveline, but she pushed her away.

"So you think forcing someone to stay with you is a good idea? I don't like bullies, Hazel, and I'd thought after what happened you wouldn't either."

Hazel winced and Aveline knew her sharply worded point had hit the bullseye.

"I don't, you're right. But these are special circumstances and I know that once you experience the life I can share with you, then you won't regret it. In fact, you'll thank me. You're intelligent and spirited and curious, Aveline, just like me, and that's why the stones sent you to me."

Behind her glasses, Aveline's eyes widened.

Bring her to me.

Signed with a letter H.

"You're the one who left the note in the stones that Harold found!"

"Maybe, maybe not," Hazel said with a sly smirk, which in Aveline's mind pretty much confirmed that she had. "But just think what's on offer here, Aveline. You'll never grow old, your bones won't ache, you'll never get sick. You can be beautiful and young for ever and all the knowledge of the world will be yours. I can't believe you're even thinking about turning this offer down."

Aveline had never seriously considered staying with Hazel before now. But as she looked into those peculiar shining eyes, she felt her own eyes growing heavy. The dazzling smile on Hazel's lips seemed to draw something out in her, an overwhelming curiosity about what this experience might actually be like. To be powerful and intelligent. To be able to move freely without the scrutiny of prying eyes. To soar through the air, the wind rushing past her like—

As the prospect wormed its way into her mind and began to seem very appealing...Aveline sensed the creeping presence of Hazel's magic and summoned the strength to resist it. What was she thinking? This wasn't what she wanted. She knew she needed to choose her next words very carefully.

"Hazel, listen, I just spoke with Alice. She said she's working on a way to grant you both peace. You just need to give her a little more time – surely that would be the best possible thing for you both?"

Hazel burst out laughing, which wasn't the response Aveline had been expecting.

"Do you really think for one moment that I *want* to be at rest?" Hazel spat. "Please don't mistake me for my short-sighted sister. Of course I still want revenge for what they did to us, but after about, ooh, a couple of hundred years, I began to realize that they'd actually done us a huge favour. Because I wasn't idle, Aveline. I continued to learn my witchcraft, only now I had time on my side. I read for years. I studied for centuries. Now I can summon storms, see the future in a trickle of water, hear the thoughts of the owl and the fox. With every passing year, I grow more powerful. I can have anything I want. Why on earth would I give all that up? The only thing I need now is someone to be here with me, so we can share these amazing things together – and I've chosen you."

"But I'm not doing it."

Hazel's eyes flickered like gas flames. "Don't speak too soon, Aveline. Strange things can happen at night. Let's just see how you feel tomorrow."

Hazel raised her hands in front of her, crossed her fingers into knots, then flung them out towards the cottage, as if she'd just thrown a handful of stones.

Then she was gone.

And Aveline knew that despite all Alice's reassurances, something bad was about to happen.

"Mugwort, way-bread, nettle, crab-apple,
thyme and fennel, the elder soap-plant.
Pound these herbs into dust,
mix with soap and with apple-dirt."

Anglo-Saxon Metrical Charm,
10th – 11th century.

Chapter 14
Magic in the Air

Running into the cottage, Aveline grabbed Harold by the sleeve.

"Quick, come with me."

"And good evening to you, too, Aveline," her mum called after her. "We're fine, thanks for asking."

Guiltily, Aveline turned around. "Sorry, Mum, just got some urgent stuff to do."

"Ach, you go right on ahead, Aveline," Mr Lieberman called from his comfy space on the sofa. "Don't worry about us, we'll still be here when you're finished."

"There's no stopping her when she's like this, Susan," Aunt Lilian chimed in. "Reminds me a little of myself. Such a smart girl."

Saved by Mr Lieberman and her aunt's timely intervention, Aveline dragged Harold into her bedroom and thrust the book that Alice had given her into his hands.

"There's a recipe in here for a witch bottle, like the one we found. It protects people from witchcraft. I need you to help me find it – now!"

Harold's face loomed pale in the lamplight. "What's happened, are we in danger?"

"Not yet, but we might be if we don't find that recipe. Hazel is a witch, Harold, and she put a spell on you, only you don't remember. I'll explain it all later, but we don't have time now."

"Righto, say no more."

As Harold began swiping through the pages, Aveline hurriedly dug out a small bottle of perfume that her mum had given her. Running across the landing to the bathroom, she gave it a quick rinse. This would be the nicest smelling witch bottle anyone had ever made. Catching sight of herself in the mirror, she narrowed her eyes and set her jaw firm.

If you want me to be a witch, Hazel, then that's what I'll be.

As she came back into the bedroom, Harold stabbed his finger at a page in the book.

"I think this is the one."

Aveline peered over his shoulder. Although the pages were faded, and the words spelled oddly, Aveline could still make sense of them.

Charme to Guarde Against Those who Meane ye Harme.

"Yep, that's it. Let me see."

In addition to a bottle, the charm called for iron filings or oak moss, neither of which Aveline had. However, the instructions also said that ground-up salt would work, too, and there was plenty of that in the kitchen. Dashing downstairs to fetch some, she forced herself to slow her pace and stroll casually through the living room.

"Just fetching a glass of water."

Back upstairs, she drizzled the salt inside the bottle. Harold watched with undisguised fascination, but refrained from asking questions, perhaps sensing that this wasn't the best time. Trailing a finger along the page, Aveline read that the charm was particularly effective if you found something personal that belonged to whoever you were trying to protect yourself against. She sat on the floor, momentarily stumped. She couldn't think of anything in the cottage that Hazel owned.

Then she remembered what the other book had said, the one Harold had brought.

To protect thyself against the witch's curse, take their Hair, and Cork it in a Bottle.

Her hairbands.

The ones Hazel had put in her hair when Aveline had stayed over.

Leaping to her feet, Aveline fetched one from her dresser and squinted at it. In amongst a couple of strands of her own hair, she could see three or four long black hairs that definitely hadn't come from her head. Carefully, she plucked them out, before twisting them between her fingers and pushing them down into the bottle. The book told her to find some sheepskin parchment to write on. Aveline had no idea if they still made stuff like that. Paper would have to do. Grabbing a pen, she wrote down what the spell suggested.

Let no witch walk where this charm lies buried.

She crammed the scrap of paper into the bottle. Just for luck, she added the old nails that came from the original bottle, feeling pleased with herself that she'd kept them. Maybe they'd add an extra level of potency?

"Um, is it working?" Harold asked.

"Not sure yet."

Everything in place, she spat in the bottle (as instructed) and gave it a shake. It didn't look particularly impressive, but then neither had the one she'd found in the garden.

She would just have to put it to the test.

"I've got to go and bury it in the garden, but I don't want my mum asking questions I can't answer. You'll have to distract her."

"Aw, no – how?"

"You'll think of something." Opening the bedroom door, she motioned Harold towards it. "Go on then, I only need two minutes."

Together, they walked downstairs and into the living room, where the adults had the TV on, but were chatting over it. Tucking the bottle behind her back, Aveline nudged Harold in the side.

"Um...what's the plan for tomorrow then?" Harold said, addressing the room a little too loudly and theatrically in Aveline's opinion. "I thought we might go out for a trip somewhere nice, maybe stop for a picnic?"

Aveline groaned inwardly.

"A picnic, Harold, really?" Aveline's mum said. "For some reason, I've never had you down as a tartan-blanket-and-sausage-roll enthusiast."

"It is most peculiar, I agree," Mr Lieberman said, running a hand through his unruly white hair. "Are you feeling okay, my boy?"

"Yes, what's wrong with liking picnics?" Harold said. "Aveline, maybe you should go and see if we have any supplies in the kitchen?"

Ah, so that's what this is all about, Aveline thought. Not the best approach, but at least it gave her a reason to leave the room. Taking her cue, she nodded.

"Good idea, Harold, I'll go and have a look."

As she ran to the back door, she heard her mum say, "Do you think these two stayed out in the sun too long today?"

Opening the door as quietly as she could and trusting that Harold would keep everybody talking for a couple of minutes, Aveline ran down the garden path. The stars sparkled like tiny silver flowers. Bending down underneath the rhododendron bush, Aveline found the hole from the old witch bottle and stuck the new one in. Looking around, she paused for a second to catch her breath.

Was Hazel watching? She didn't think so. Aveline could normally sense when she was near. Besides, even if she was, what could she do? The bottle now lay safely in the ground.

It was done.

Back inside, Harold was still doing a very poor job of convincing everybody that he wanted to go for a picnic. Taking a seat, Aveline let the conversation wash over her. She wasn't sure what Hazel had planned, but she could feel trouble brewing. Her skin tingled, as if someone was trailing a cold fork over her arms. Strange thoughts whirled around her mind like dizzy moths. The hot summer made the air heavy and thick every evening, but tonight it felt like soup, each breath having to be gulped down.

Outside, Aveline heard a shrill shriek. It could have been a fox. Or a cat. But Aveline suspected not and gripped the edge of her seat so tightly that her knuckles showed white beneath her skin.

"What was that?"

"What was what, my love?" Aveline's mum replied.

"That noise."

"I didn't hear anything myself, dear," Mr Lieberman

said, tapping his ear with one finger. "Though my hearing isn't what it was."

"Harold?" Aveline asked. "Did you hear it?"

A shake of his shaggy fringe told her no. But she hadn't imagined it. Getting up, she walked to the kitchen window and pulled herself up onto the sink to peer out.

Hazel stood just beyond the open garden gate, rubbing the ball of her foot. When she saw Aveline, she raised a finger and wagged it to and fro. A moment later, Aveline heard Hazel's voice.

Oh, Aveline, I see you've been making charms. Who taught you that? Let me guess…Alice? You could have warned me – that hurt.

Only, the voice wasn't coming from Hazel, whose lips were locked in a thin, mocking smile. It came from inside Aveline's head.

"Leave us alone," Aveline whispered.

Slowly, Hazel shook her head.

Let's see what the night brings first.

"Who are you talking to, Aveline?" her mum called from the living room.

"No one."

Dropping her feet to the floor, Aveline made her way into the living room. Now she'd made Hazel angry and the thought of dealing with a vengeful witch made her blood run cold. More terrifying still, Hazel had also found some way to get inside her head. Maybe this wasn't the first time? She recalled when she'd breezily agreed to go to Hazel's without Harold. Had Hazel got inside her head then, too? What else could Hazel make her do – stay in Norton Wick for ever? Aveline's heart thudded and she could feel a cold panic spreading through her like ice water. Taking off her glasses, she took a deep breath and remembered the witch bottle, which was now safely buried in the soil. At least that seemed to have gone perfectly to plan. Hazel couldn't get close to them. So what could she really do from a distance?

As if to answer her question, a gust of wind rattled the windows. A moment later there was another, this one fiercer than the last so that the cottage seemed to tremble. A roof tile smashed on the ground outside. The bins blew over with a loud crash. The shadows of waving branches danced on the walls like skeletal fingers. Every door in the house began to slam open and shut, as if wrenched angrily by invisible hands.

It appeared Aveline was about to find out just exactly what Hazel could do.

As Aveline stood tense and alert, she saw to her

surprise that nobody else had reacted. They sat with their chins resting on their chests, as if they'd slipped into an evening snooze.

Hazel had done it again.

She'd bewitched the cottage and everybody in it, all except Aveline.

Aveline was on her own.

As quickly as the doors had begun banging on their hinges, they stopped. The winds that had briefly raged ceased, too. The cottage held its breath, waiting for what would happen next.

That was when Aveline saw the smoke.

It trailed in from the fireplace like a serpent. Thick coils of a rotten yellow hue, like something she'd seen belching out of the chimney at a particularly unpleasant factory.

It looked exactly like something a witch might conjure.

"Fair is foul and foul is fair,
hover through the fog and filthy air."

The Three Witches, Macbeth,
Act 1 Scene 1.

Chapter 15

"Oh, She's a Crafty One"

Transfixed, Aveline could only watch aghast as the smoke slithered over the cottage floor, the stench of sulphur clogging her nostrils. Holding her breath, she ran to the fireplace, looking around for something to block it with. Logs had been left to one side in a wicker basket, all ready for autumn. Aveline tried placing them in the fireplace like building blocks, but it did nothing to stop the steady stream of smoke. Grabbing a pile of old newspapers from the kindling basket, she began stuffing them up into the chimney.

"Aveline, whatever are you doing?"

Turning, Aveline saw her mum glaring at her. While apparently awake now, her mum didn't seem to notice the thick yellow smoke that snaked its way up her legs and wrapped itself around her waist. And it appeared she'd woken in a foul mood.

"Get away from there and stop messing about with the fireplace! I don't know, why are you always up to something every time my back's turned?"

"Because she's a sneak, that's why." As Aunt Lilian came to stand beside her mum, Aveline was horrified to see a sneer of displeasure on her aunt's face. "You just see, it'll get her into trouble one day. Children like her always tend to come to a sticky end."

They both spoke in a tone that Aveline had never heard before – angry, vicious and spiteful…as if they *hated* her.

"B-but, it's this smoke," Aveline stammered. "Can't you see it?"

"Making things up again, Aveline?" Harold, too, had woken from his second supernatural snooze and angrily flung his hair out of his eyes. "Just like your ghosts and witches. You don't actually believe any of that, do you? It's all about you trying to be the centre of attention."

"Harold!" Aveline gasped. How could he be so mean? Was that what he really thought about her?

"I think the boy is right on this occasion," Mr Lieberman piped up. "I'd recommend sending her away to boarding school, Susan. They don't stand for any nonsense at those places."

"And what would you know about it?" Aunt Lilian snarled at him. "Harold's no example, always running amok and doing as he pleases."

"I can do what I like, you're not my mum," Harold bit back.

"Didn't you teach him *anything* while his parents were spending all their money on your private lessons?" Now Aveline's mum turned her attention to Aunt Lilian. "Some tutor you are! If it was me, I'd ask for a refund."

"You've always been jealous of me," Aunt Lilian said. "I was the one with the brains and you've never forgiven me for it."

"Ha! Jealous of you? Don't make me laugh!" Aveline's mum spat back at Aunt Lilian.

"I wish I'd never come on this stupid holiday," Harold cried.

"See what you've gone and done now, Aveline!" her mum yelled, her face twisted and red. "All this is because of you. Why do you constantly have to spoil everything?"

Aveline's face flushed and she blinked as tears welled in her eyes. It was true. It *was* all her fault. She'd been the one to bring danger to their doorstep. If she hadn't gone chasing around after Hazel, none of this would have happened.

Deep inside, a chilling thought came to Aveline. Was this what Hazel's dark magic could do? Had it given her the means to see what her loved ones truly thought of her – and each other? Was this what people were really like? Seething with bitterness and resentment?

Right on cue, she heard Hazel's voice in her head. *You see, Aveline? I'm the only one you can trust. I'll never treat you badly.*

Digging her hands deep into her pockets, Aveline gulped and bowed her head, trying to shut out the awful din of insults and accusations that raged around her. All she wanted to do now was escape the cottage and go somewhere quiet and calm. The cool trail of a tear ran over her cheek. Hazel's offer to escape all this was suddenly becoming very tempting.

Then, in her pocket, she felt something.

A small, wiry bundle.

The herbs Alice had given her.

She'd told Aveline they might come in handy, and right now Aveline didn't have any other options. Ignoring the angry shouts that filled the room as everybody continued yelling at her and each other, Aveline found a box of matches by the fireplace and struck one. Holding it to the leafy bundle, she let the tips catch before blowing them out and letting them smoulder. Thick white smoke rose into the air and, at the same time, a strong herbal fragrance filled the room.

Immediately, the sinister vapour on the cottage floor began to disperse, retreating hastily back into the fireplace as if being chased. Wafting the herby bundle as furiously as she could, Aveline began to walk around the room, realizing to her delight that everybody had stopped yelling and was now watching her with puzzled frowns, as if they'd just woken up from a long sleep – which in one sense they had.

"That smells...amazing, my love," Aveline's mum said, taking a big sniff. "Where did you get it?"

"A friend gave it to me."

Continuing to wave it around like a sparkler on Bonfire Night, Aveline watched out of the corner of her eye as the yellow smoke scuttled back up the chimney. Everybody yawned in unison, and Mr Lieberman ran a hand through his hair.

"I seem to have become very tired all of a sudden. This country air and exercise must be doing me some good."

"Me too," Aunt Lilian said. "That lovely incense you're burning is making me feel incredibly relaxed, Aveline. I might have a hot drink and then bed."

"I'm pretty exhausted, too," Aveline's mum said. "Well, it seems we're all decided – bedtime it is. What a wonderful day it's been."

As everybody began to gather their things, Harold came and stood by Aveline's shoulder and breathed in through his nostrils.

"Reminds me of my dad's aftershave," he said.

"Just keep sniffing," Aveline said. "You wouldn't believe what was happening in here a few minutes ago."

"You know, I sort of remember feeling angry with you

226

for some reason," Harold replied. "I thought I was having a bad dream, but then I woke up and you were waving that stuff around." His face blanched. "Oh no, it was something to do with Hazel, wasn't it?"

"Yes, she was trying to turn you all against me."

"She needs to try harder then."

And with that, Harold gave her a huge grin, which right at that moment felt like the most wonderful thing in the world. As the adults hobbled and yawned their way upstairs, Aveline left the smouldering herbs on the corner of the brick fireplace, where they slowly burned out.

"See, Hazel? I know a few tricks, too," Aveline whispered.

She waited to see if she would hear a reply, but there was only silence. Maybe Hazel had given up for tonight – not that Aveline thought Hazel was finished with her yet. And with a week of their holiday still to go, Aveline knew she would have to act. They couldn't stay locked up in the cottage under the protection of the witch bottle for ever, and she didn't have the expertise to fight magical battles every night. Although she'd won one small victory tonight, there would be more challenges to come. But she'd already thought ahead and had a plan – and for that she'd need to be up early, which meant bed for her, too.

She suddenly felt worn out. Witchcraft, it seemed, was hard work.

"Goodnight, Aveline, I love you," Aveline's mum called as she heard her come up to bed.

"Love you, too, Mum," Aveline replied, and she meant every word.

Did Hazel really think she would give all this up? Hazel had seriously underestimated her.

The next morning, Aveline reached for her mobile before its alarm woke the whole house. Dressing quickly, she crept downstairs, where she was relieved to see Harold waiting, bouncing around on his toes as if warming up to play football. She'd told him the plan before they'd gone to bed and he'd insisted on coming too, despite the early hour.

"Don't suppose we've got time for a fried-egg sandwich?" he asked hopefully.

"'Fraid not," Aveline said, even though her stomach rumbled. For once, she had something more important to do than eating.

They unlatched the back door as quietly as they could and checked the coast was clear.

"Do you think it's safe to leave the house?" Harold asked.

"Probably not," Aveline said. "We'll need to be quick."

They made their way through the garden and out towards the middle of The Witch Stones. One or two stars could still be seen, but the horizon was steadily growing brighter. Sunrise wasn't far away. Thick morning mist covered the ground, so the stones appeared to be floating in the clouds. Never had they looked more magical – which was good, Aveline thought, because magic was what they'd come here to do.

If you give the stones something, you get something in return.

The night before, Aveline had done a quick itinerary of all her possessions, which had turned out to be quite depressing in truth. She didn't really own anything that might be considered precious. She'd already cashed in her bracelet. But she did have the dolphin pendant that Hazel had conjured up and, in a way, it seemed an appropriate gift to leave. This was her saying goodbye.

Hazel wanted more than Aveline could ever give her, and when friendships went sour, sometimes it was best to just get away somewhere quiet and keep your head down for a while. Which was why Aveline had written on a slip of paper: *Please get us safely home today*.

She rolled it up and squeezed it into a crevice in one of the stones. Beside it, on the grass, she lay the pendant down.

"What did you bring?" Aveline asked Harold. She'd decided it would be better to err on the side of generosity and had told Harold to bring something valuable, too.

Reluctantly, he pulled out his binoculars and laid them gently beside her pendant.

"Goodbye, old spyglasses, you've served me well."

"I'll get you some more for your birthday, I promise."

"It's okay, I want to get away from here in one piece, too. So, what happens now? Do we have to hold hands and dance around or something?"

"I don't know. Run back and have some breakfast?"

Aveline looked around. In truth, she'd wanted something dramatic to happen – for the mist to suddenly clear and the birds to start singing. Which made her realize it did seem unusually quiet, even for early morning. As Aveline listened, her skin rippled in response to something more than just the cool dew of the dawn mist. Something *was* happening. The mist swirled and churned. The earth beneath them seemed to tremble for an instant.

At first Aveline thought it was her own heartbeat she could hear.

A dull *thud-thud-thud*.

But then it began to get louder.

The sound of a drum.

A dull, hollow thud. Something ancient. Bone on animal skin.

"Who's banging a drum at this time of the morning?" Harold whispered.

"I don't know, but I think we should get going."

"Agreed."

They began to walk, very quickly, back towards the cottage. Intuition told them that this was no time for idle curiosity. Only, as they hurriedly walked away across the field, the drumming appeared to be coming from in front of them. They did an about-turn, but the same thing happened again. No matter which direction they headed in, the drum sounded louder and closer and more threatening, and as they changed direction, and changed direction again, Aveline realized that they were being herded like sheep towards the centre of the circle.

The drum picked up its pace, the rhythmic thud making their heads throb. The mist swirled, giving the strange impression that the stones were circling them like sharks around a fishing boat.

"Look," Harold said.

But Aveline had already seen them.

Silhouettes in the mist.

Ghostly grey shrouded figures, moving quickly and silently nearer.

They were surrounded, the figures closing in around them to make a tight circle. The drumming stopped, and Aveline heard Harold gasp.

"Oh no."

"You're going to pay for this."

Hazel Browne, Witch Trial,
Norton Wick, 1653.

Chapter 16

Escape Plans

"They're witches!" Harold panted. "They're witches and they've come for us!"

Aveline grabbed Harold by the arm. The silhouetted figures appeared to have strange spikes sticking up out of their heads. Aveline's first thought was that they were wearing pointed hats, like the ones people wear when they dress up as witches on Halloween – though one thing she'd learned since coming to Norton Wick was that real witches didn't go in for that type of stuff. Then the figures drew in even closer, like hyenas circling their prey. There appeared to be around eight or nine of them. Their clothing was ragged. They seemed wild, almost feral, and Aveline saw bare, skinny limbs on which strange blue spirals had been painted or tattooed. Their movements were cautious and stealthy, yet graceful, too; they were almost catlike in the way they moved between the stones. Aveline weighed up the pros and cons of calling for help. It was still early and with the muffling effects of the fog, it seemed unlikely anybody would hear. Also, she wasn't wholly convinced that Harold was right about them being witches.

"Your mate Hazel has summoned her friends to come and get us," Harold insisted. "We need to run. Like, now."

"Wait a minute," Aveline whispered, slowly letting go of Harold's arm. "I'm not even sure they can see us."

While the figures were menacing in appearance, they'd made no threatening moves towards Harold and Aveline. If anything, they seemed to be ignoring them completely, focused solely on the stones, as if they existed in another time and place. As the figures edged closer, Aveline realized the strange spikes she'd seen were actually matted strands of hair, made stiff with mud or dung, before being twisted skywards. Some of the figures wore necklaces and wristbands, decorated with amulets and bones, which clinked together as they moved. Now they could see the drummer, a slender woman with a striking white scar running from forehead to chin. Under her elbow, she clasped a small drum tight to her ribs, tapping it rhythmically with what looked like a wooden rattle.

"Oh my," Aveline said quietly. "I think they might be druids."

Harold peered at her with a curled lip. "Are you sure? They don't look anything like that bloke on the pub sign."

"I think so. They haven't come for us, look, they've come for the offerings we left."

Aveline's fears slowly melted away to be replaced by a sense of relief. It felt the same as when she'd burned the herbs the night before, a calming presence that spread through her limbs like warm water. These were the druids of legend. The mysterious inhabitants of stone circles and mistletoe groves. Aveline realized that she and Harold weren't in danger. These people, or spirits, hadn't come to harm them.

They'd come because they'd been called.

She'd summoned them to the stones.

As Aveline and Harold held their breath, a druid scurried towards the stone where they'd left their message stuffed inside a crack. Small and wiry, with dark eyes that sparkled with curiosity, he ran his hand reverently over the surface, before crouching and examining the note together with the gifts they'd left. Harold's binoculars seemed to be particularly fascinating, and the man turned them over and over in his hands. Then, turning back towards the assembled druids, he raised one hand to the sky. As one, the others raised theirs, too. They began to hum as the drummer picked up the beat. Aveline felt her heart thump in perfect time.

"I think they've accepted our gifts," Aveline whispered.

"Good, those binoculars cost me twenty quid," Harold said.

The humming grew louder, like a swarm of bees. Aveline gasped as strands of silver and emerald light snaked out of the stone and began to swirl over and around them. Like a rope knotting itself together, the bands of light twisted and spiralled until it seemed as if they'd stepped into another universe, one where the sky was made of jewelled ribbons. Aveline placed a hand on her cheek, as if to reassure herself that she still existed. She felt like she was floating through time, her head light and giddy, her chest heaving as all the breaths she'd been holding rushed out as one. A gust of wind fluttered on her cheek like a kiss and she saw that the bands of light were wrapping around them both, until they were enclosed in a sparkling cocoon that was warm and magical and soothing.

After the dark, tangled magic of the previous night, it felt like a gulp of cool, clear water on a parched throat, and Aveline's fear of Hazel slowly faded away.

Finally, the bands of light drifted up into the air like woodsmoke. The druids dropped their arms, the hum died away and they bowed their heads as the drummer slowed and then stopped. For the briefest moment, Aveline and Harold looked up to see the druids staring back at them with expressions that could have been either curiosity or confusion. Aveline couldn't resist grinning at them and stifled a delighted laugh. But before she had time to say anything, the mists quickly thickened, swirling around the mystical figures until stone and human became indistinguishable, and Aveline and Harold found themselves alone once again. They stayed where they were, each of them filled with a light-headed sense of wonder that both of them wished to savour. How long they stood there, Aveline didn't know, but she suddenly realized that the mists had gone and the golden rays of a late summer sunrise were warming their skin.

"Let's just keep this between you and me," Aveline said finally.

"Fine by me," Harold said in a croaky voice. "Nobody would believe us anyway. I'm not even sure I believe it myself. Maybe it was something to do with not eating breakfast."

Grinning, Aveline pulled him lightly by the arm towards the stone where they'd left their request. They took a few moments to examine the ground where they'd set down the pendant and the binoculars.

They'd disappeared.

Just like the note they'd put in the stones, too.

"So, do you think we're home and dry?" Harold said. "I don't know about you, but I don't feel half as scared as I did an hour ago."

"I hope so," Aveline replied. "But I won't feel fully safe until we've driven past the sign that says *Welcome to Norton Wick*."

"Let's go then, get something to eat. Meeting ghost druids always makes me hungry."

As they walked back across the field, rabbits romped ahead of them and skylarks wheeled above, swooping and soaring like Aveline's spirits. When they reached the cottage, Aveline's mum was standing on the doorstep, cradling a steaming mug of tea.

"I wondered where you two had got to. I have bad news, I'm afraid," she called. "The owner of the cottage has just called. She's doubled-booked us by mistake and wanted to know if there was any chance of getting the cottage back earlier. She was incredibly apologetic and has offered to refund us in full, but the poor dear sounded so upset I said we could leave today and not to worry about it. I'm sorry, I know this is your holiday, but do you think you could get packed?"

"Oh no, that's a shame," Harold said, flashing Aveline a wide-eyed look of disbelief. "Yes, I mean, it'll only take me five minutes to get my gear together."

"Are you sure, Mum? It feels like we only just got here," Aveline added, trying to disguise the joy that warmed her cheeks.

"I'm truly sorry, but she was so upset about it, and apparently these other guests are coming from a long way away. I'll make it up to you both, I promise."

"Oh well, I suppose we'd best go get our stuff," Aveline said.

Upstairs, Aveline and Harold crammed everything they'd brought into their bags and did a happy dance.

"We did it, Harold!"

"Escape from Norton Wick – level unlocked," Harold said, pretending to buff his fingernails on his T-shirt. "Wow, can you believe it? We've just summoned ancient druids and successfully conducted a magical ritual!

Normally it's a good day if I successfully conduct myself out of bed. I have to say, Aveline, while being with you is never boring, part of me thinks I'd prefer a holiday without witches and dead druids. You know, just sitting on a beach, swimming in the sea, reading a book, playing games on my phone, like normal people do."

"Don't lie, you like it really."

"I suppose I must," Harold said with a floppy grin.

"It is a shame, in a way, having to leave," Aveline said, looking at her shoes. "It does feel like you've only just arrived."

"Yeah, I know what you mean. And part of me isn't quite ready for a lecture on the history of every single place we happen to pass in the car on the way home. But I suppose that's better than being chased by an angry witch. Anyway, we're not out of here yet."

They could hear the adults packing, too, and shortly after they all congregated by the front door and began loading up the cars. Aveline was going to go home with her mum, while Mr Lieberman, Aunt Lilian and Harold would make the trip back down to Malmouth.

"See you both soon," Aunt Lilian said, before giving Aveline and her mum a hug and sliding into the driving seat. "I'm sorry we couldn't spend more time together, but we'll make up for it next time."

"Ach, it appears I've been relegated to co-pilot again," Mr Lieberman said. "So nice to see you both, thank you for having us and please come down to Malmouth again at your earliest convenience."

"We will," Aveline's mum said. "Take care and drive safely."

"Laters," Harold said, giving Aveline a thumbs up. "Send me a text when you get back."

"Will do," Aveline said. "And thanks for bringing the books, I think they saved the day."

"Let's see if we make it home first," Harold answered with a grin, before giving her a quick hug and climbing into the back seat, where he immediately pressed his face and hands against the glass like he did when he arrived.

"You've done that joke once already," Aveline said, miming a yawn.

Harold shrugged as the car pulled away. Aveline waved until it was out of sight, suddenly feeling a little lonely. That made her think of Hazel.

"You know, Aveline, whenever you and Harold get together it's like you're speaking a different language. What was all that talk about saving the day?"

"Oh, we were just joking around."

"Wish I understood the punchline. Something makes me think you and I had very different holiday experiences."

Aveline smiled as her mum's soft curls shook from laughing. If only her mum knew how right she was. As she was about to climb in the car, Aveline's mum gestured to the front gate.

"Looks like you've got a visitor," Mum said. "Don't be long, love, we've got to get going."

Aveline knew who it was before she even looked.

Hazel stood underneath the apple tree, hands stuffed in jeans pockets, kicking pebbles into the dusty road. In one hand she held the reins to her glamorous horse, which gave a disinterested snort. Glancing up, she looked at Aveline and smiled. Nothing wicked or malicious. Just a shy grin that made Aveline's heart ache just a little bit.

"Hi, Hazel," Aveline said, walking over to the gate.

"So, you're off then," Hazel said, giving the dust one final kick. "Thought you were here for a few more days yet?"

"We were, only we've had to leave the cottage. Something came up suddenly."

"Strange, that."

"Yep, just like last night. That was pretty strange, too."

"Seems my plan didn't work then."

"It was a pretty horrible thing to do."

"Witches are wicked, didn't you know?"

For a moment neither of them knew what to say. Eventually, Aveline held out her hand.

"See you then."

Hazel paused, before reaching out and giving Aveline's hand a squeeze.

"Yes," Hazel said, her eyes glittering as they caught the sun. "Maybe sooner than you think."

Aveline laughed, a little nervously, before yanking her hand away. Then, without another word, she walked to the car, climbed in and buckled herself up.

"Don't worry, you'll see her again," Aveline's mum said. "We can come back any time you like."

Not a chance, Aveline thought, but left it at that.

As her mum nursed their car out onto the narrow, winding country lane that led out of Norton Wick, Aveline breathed a sigh of relief. Yet as she wound down the window to let in some much-needed air, a black blur behind the hedgerows made her jerk up in alarm. In the field beyond, Hazel galloped parallel to the car. It looked like she was trying to keep pace with them. Even from a distance, Aveline could see the look of grim determination on Hazel's face. In that instant, her insides turned to jelly. She should have known better. Hazel wouldn't give up so easily. And while they were still in Norton Wick, they were still in danger.

"Is that Hazel on the horse? Should I stop?" her mum asked.

Biting her lip, Aveline looked for the sign that marked the end of Norton Wick, but couldn't see it quite yet.

"Um, no, keep going, she's just showing off."

Aveline risked another glance. Hazel had stood up in her stirrups. Releasing one hand from the reins, she began to make a series of strange gestures in their direction. Ahead of them, a row of elm trees lined the road. Leaves began to flutter down onto the car, as if autumn had begun a little early.

"Best get a move on, Mum, so we can get back and unpack," Aveline said.

"I can only go twenty miles an hour on these lanes and I'm not breaking the speed limit," her mum replied.

Through the open window, Aveline could hear the dull thump of the horse's hooves as it tore across the grass, its head tossing wildly, the sun shining on its black flanks. Above that, Aveline thought she could hear Hazel's voice, crying out words that she couldn't quite understand.

Gripping the sides of her seat, Aveline saw shimmering bands of colour snake between the branches of the trees, the same ones that she'd seen that morning in the circle. The trees swayed. Leaves rained down like a shower of yellow confetti, forcing Hazel away from the car, until Aveline lost sight of her behind a hedge.

"Whatever's going on with the weather?" Aveline's mum said, gripping the steering wheel a little tighter.

Aveline jumped again as something brilliantly white flew close over the car. A magnificent spread of ivory feathers. A heart-shaped face. Black eyes. A set of cruel-looking talons stretched in flight.

"Oh my, would you look at that!" Aveline's mum said, stepping on the brakes.

"It's a barn owl," Aveline said, trying to follow its flight while keeping one eye on where Hazel had got to.

"I know," her mum said excitedly, turning her head to peer after it. "Flown off somewhere. Well I never, it's rare to see one in the daytime. Maybe this weather disturbed it."

They turned their attention back to the road. The owl had distracted Aveline for a moment. Her eyes darted left and right as she tried to see where Hazel had gone. There was magic in the air. She could feel it, surrounding the car like a force field. The druids were on her side and it gave her confidence.

Yet as they rounded a curve, Aveline saw her. Somehow, Hazel had managed to get ahead of them. Now she blocked the road, sitting astride her horse, which blew steam from its nostrils like a dragon. Aveline's mum slowed almost to a stop.

"Whatever is she doing?"

"I don't know."

"Did you forget something?"

"No."

Hazel wheeled the horse around in a tight circle, glaring at them as they approached. Just over Hazel's shoulder, Aveline could see the signpost that marked the boundary of the village. Their car had almost come to a halt, and Aveline was desperately trying to decide how to handle the situation. The way forward was blocked. They would have to stop. But what would she do? More importantly, what did Hazel plan to do? Aveline crossed her fingers and hoped that druid magic would beat witch magic.

Just then, Hazel's horse reared as the barn owl wheeled past again in a white blur. Hazel was flung back in the saddle. A look of alarm flashed across her face as she clutched at the reins. Aveline's mum stopped the car and quickly unlatched her seat belt.

"Quick, we need to help her, her horse is about to bolt."

But even as Aveline unbuckled herself and prepared to get out, a figure ran out of the hedgerow where the owl had disappeared, and grabbed Hazel's horse firmly by the reins.

"It's okay," Aveline whispered. "Alice is there."

"Where did she appear from?"

"I have no idea," Aveline said, despite having a *very* good idea what had happened.

Immediately the horse reared again, kicking out its forelegs. Aveline and her mum gasped in unison, sensing that they might be about to witness a terrible accident. But while Alice's hat flew off, after a few moments she managed to soothe the horse and bring it under control, stroking its cheeks and whispering in its ear, before leading it to the side of the road. Hazel dismounted and wagged a finger furiously in Alice's direction. While not quite shouting, they appeared to be having a very heated conversation. Aveline couldn't quite catch what was being said, but it didn't look like they were exchanging sisterly advice.

Aveline's mum drove slowly towards them.

"Everything okay?" she called out of the car window.

Alice turned and started to speak before coughing and pulling something from her mouth. Something small and white. A feather. She flicked it away and it fluttered to the floor. Aveline wondered if her mum had noticed.

"We're fine, thank you," Alice replied. "Hazel's horse just got a little startled. Sorry about that, it's safe to drive past now. Are you leaving us already?"

"Yes, I'm afraid we've had to depart in something of a hurry, but we'll see you again, I'm sure – we're only down the road!" Aveline's mum called.

"Blessed be then," Alice said with a nod of her head, before looking past Aveline's mum to where Aveline sat, fiddling with her seat belt. "Take care, Aveline, and thank you for being so nice to Hazel."

After they'd driven past, Aveline took one last glance out of the back window and saw Hazel climb back onto her horse. For a second, Hazel turned in the saddle, those uncanny eyes meeting Aveline's. Hazel smiled. Or sneered. Aveline couldn't tell which. Then they turned a corner and Hazel was gone.

"Alice and Hazel's relationship is a little unusual, don't you think?" Aveline's mum said, mercifully speeding up a little. "They're almost like mother and daughter."

Close, but not quite right, Aveline thought, before turning her attention back to the road and the Norton Wick sign. As they passed it, she breathed a sigh of relief. She almost wanted to reach out and give it a hug. Pushing herself down into her seat, she turned her face to the window, closed her eyes and let the cool breeze wash over her. It felt like a refreshing shower after a long day doing hard and dirty work.

Aveline's wish had come true, sort of. She'd wanted to discover more about the standing stones and the legends attached to them. But never in her wildest dreams had she thought a real-life witch – two of them, in fact – would come into her life in such an abrupt and explosive way. Not to mention meeting the druids, which had already begun to feel like the weirdest dream ever.

She wondered how Harold was feeling. Like her, he'd be sitting in a car, probably running through everything in his head and trying to make sense of it. What an adventure it had been.

Aveline couldn't help feeling as if she'd just had a very lucky escape. Sighing, she opened her eyes and saw that the narrow lanes had turned into wide roads, which meant they were heading away from the countryside and back towards the city.

"You okay, love?" her mum said. "I hope you're not too sad about having to go home early."

"Oh, you know, it's a shame we couldn't stay a little longer," Aveline said, hiding a smile. In truth she wanted to scream with relief.

"Don't worry, we can go somewhere else, just as soon as work quietens down a little. Maybe when your next half-term break comes along."

"That'd be great, Mum."

"We could go and stay near another stone circle, if you like, seeing as how they're your new favourite subject?"

"Maybe," Aveline said, before finishing the sentence in her head.

Maybe not.

The End

Turn on your torches and join
Aveline Jones in her next adventure

Aveline is determined to discover the truth behind her uncle's mysterious disappearance when she travels to his home with Mum and Aunt Lilian. After years of hoping Aveline's uncle would return, they have finally decided to sell his house – but Aveline and Harold have other plans.

Sneaking into her uncle's study, Aveline discovers he had been investigating possible supernatural activity around an ancient burial mound – and linked this with the unexplained disappearances of other local villagers.

But when Aveline and Harold embark on a trip to the burial mound, they find themselves captured by dark, magical forces…and trapped somewhere no one will ever find them. Can they make it out alive?

Find out in
The Vanishing of Aveline Jones
COMING SOON